BABCOCK

Joe Cottonwood

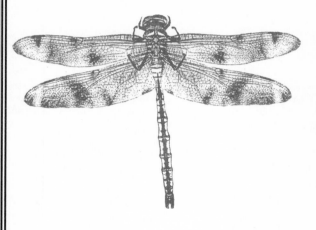

SCHOLASTIC PRESS

NEW YORK

Library of Congress Cataloging-in-Publication Data

Cottonwood, Joe.
Babcock / Joe Cottonwood.
p. cm.
Summary: Babcock, a seventh-grade black boy who likes
dragonflies, poetry, and music, falls in love with Kirsten, a blonde,
at the same time that Uncle Earl moves in with his family.
ISBN 0-590-22221-X
[1. Love — Fiction. 2. Friendship — Fiction. 3. Uncles — Fiction.
4. Afro-Americans — Fiction.]
I. Title.
PZ7. C8296Bab   1995
[Fic] — dc20   95-15549
CIP   AC

12 11 10 9 8 7 6 5 4 3 2 1   6 7 8 9/9 0 1/0

Printed in the U.S.A.   37
First printing, October 1996

✦

I loved my friend.
He went away from me.
There is nothing more to say.
The poem ends,
Soft as it began —
I loved my friend.

— *Langston Hughes*

LEGS

I was throwing popcorn to some ducks.

Suddenly a pair of legs — human legs — went flying in front of my face.

"Hey," I said.

"Hey, yourself," said the owner of the legs. She was a skinny white girl with blonde hair and freckles — thousands of freckles. Big ears. She was my age. She went to my school. She hung out with two other girls who always turned their backs and giggled whenever anybody walked by — or at least, whenever *I* walked by.

I don't like to be giggled at.

She stood up straight as if she was trying to stretch that skinny body until it was thin as a noodle, and then she turned a handspring — and again, her legs flew in front of my face.

I said, "Could you do that somewhere else?"

She stood facing me. Then, instead of answering me, she giggled — and did another handspring.

I said, "I was here first."

"You don't own this pond," she said. "Although I do see you here practically every day. What are you doing, anyway?"

"Never mind." I wasn't going to try to explain to some giggler about how I spent my life. I did spend a part of most days at the lake: feeding ducks, watching frogs, talking to dragonflies. I like animals.

She tossed her blonde hair out of her face and said, "Would you move somewhere else?" Though it was a request, she spoke with the assurance of someone who was used to getting her way — because she was a girl. Because she was blonde. Because some people would think she was cute. "The moss grows here," she said. "And the ground is so soft." She bounced up and down on her toes. "It's springy — like a big mat. So would you please move?"

I felt a twitching on my upper lip. When I feel that twitching, I smile. People who know me — who've seen my regular smile — know to watch out for this one. Boone told me once that it makes me look dead, like a smile that an undertaker put on my face. It's a warning — if you recognize it.

"No," I said. Of course, I could have moved. I could throw popcorn to ducks anywhere around the pond. But I don't like to be pushed. Not by bullies. And not by skinny girls who giggle at me in school. And now my upper lip was twitching, and I was showing the undertaker smile, but she didn't know what it meant.

"Well," she said, "I guess there's room enough for both of us here."

"No."

She looked at me with surprise. She frowned. But instead of arguing, she turned three cartwheels in a triangular pattern that brought her right back in front of me.

She brushed some hair out of her face. "See? We can share."

"No."

She stared at me, looking partly puzzled and partly hurt, as if she was wondering, Why are you acting so nasty to me when I'm so cute?

She held her hands up near her head in preparation for turning another cartwheel or handspring or doubleflip gymnastics razzledazzle whatever when suddenly an orange dragonfly — who should have known better — zipped out of nowhere, hovered for just a moment in front of her face, and landed on her shoulder.

For a split second she looked down at that dragonfly. And in that split second I was thinking, Maybe she's all right, after all. Maybe the dragonflies know something I don't know about her.

"Yech!" she shouted, and she slapped her shoulder. The dragonfly cracked into slime and fell dead at her feet. "Ugh," she said, curling her lip. "Ee-uw. *Gross*. Now I've got *insect guts* on my *hand.*" She shook it in the air.

That's when it happened. I didn't mean to trip her. I didn't mean to do anything except flip the dead dragonfly away with the toe of my shoe while ducking my head so she couldn't see the wetness brimming in my eyes, but all of a sudden she shifted her feet thisaway just as my leg went thataway, and we both lost our balance and fell to the ground, and some things are just instinct — because I was angry, you know, and I've fought with boys plenty of times who

4

thought they could bully me, and it always came out the same, with me on top, and here I'd fallen accidentally and it just . . . well . . . I was sitting on her.

She flailed her legs. She screamed: "Let me *up,* you big fat *slob!*"

"Promise you'll go away," I said.

"You're just *jealous* because you can't do a *cartwheel,*" she shouted. "Because you're too *fat.*" She was punching me.

"At least I'm not skinny," I said. "You're flat as a board."

"Don't call me flat!"

"Don't call me fat."

"You *are* fat. Fat! Fat! Fat!"

"You aren't even blonde," I said. "You're a fake."

"I am *not* a fake."

"Your eyebrows are dark. You dyed your hair."

"I did *not.* They're just different colors." She stopped flailing her legs and punching my side. In a hurt voice, she said, "Don't make fun of the way I look."

"You started it."

"*I* started it? You tripped me. You're sitting on me."

"You called me fat."

"Well. You *are* fat."

I was starting to feel uncomfortable. What was I doing? How would it look to somebody passing by? I was too old to be fighting with a girl.

"This is unbearable," she said. "Would you please let me up?"

"Will you go away?"

"No."

The anger had gone out of me. The dragonfly was dead. That was that. And as for what she'd said about me — I wasn't thinking about what she'd said. Instead, I was noticing what she *hadn't* said. She'd been angry; she'd said the most awful thing she could think of to try to hurt me; she was white; I was black, and she'd called me fat. That's all. Just fat.

I stood up, reached out a hand, and helped pull her to her feet.

"I'm sorry," I said.

She didn't say anything. She was standing with her head bowed and her hands on her hips.

"I shouldn't have done that," I said.

She didn't say anything.

"Are you all right?"

She didn't answer.

"Would you please say something?"

Speaking to the ground, she said, "It's not fair, you know. I can't help it if I'm skinny. I can't help it if my eyebrows are the wrong color. I can't help it if my ears are too big and I have too many freckles. You shouldn't say that."

"I didn't say anything about ears and freckles."

She looked up at me. "You were *going* to."

"No. I wasn't." What amazed me was, she didn't think she was cute. I was all wrong about her. I felt confused. I was looking into her eyes: blue, flashing, like sun on water. What had we been fighting about, anyway? I felt dizzy. I said, "I happen to like big ears. And freckles."

She narrowed her eyes. But then she set her jaw with determination and said, "You lost, you know. You beat me up, but you lost."

"I didn't beat you up."

"You tripped me. You sat on me."

"I didn't beat you up. I didn't hit you. Not once. *You* were hitting *me*. I bet I didn't even hurt you."

"You hurt my feelings."

"I said I was sorry."

"You fought. And you lost."

She was standing in front of me. She knew

she had just as much right to stand there as I did. Oh yeah — *that's* what we'd been fighting about. And she'd proved that I couldn't intimidate her. I'd lost my temper, and then she'd lost hers, and we'd shouted some things that now we wished we hadn't said, and we both were still here. Now I felt bad. I felt *guilty*. I felt big and awkward and stupid. I felt like a bully. She was right. I'd lost.

"Truce?" I said.

She looked me right in the eye. "My name's Kirsten."

"I know," I said. "My name's Babcock."

"I know," she said.

It's funny how you can go to the same school, and some people you get to know and maybe you like them and maybe you don't, and other people you just know by name, and it can stay that way for years until suddenly something happens. And it just happened.

"What made you so mad?" she asked.

"You killed a dragonfly."

"You like *bugs?*"

"Yes."

She stared at me. She looked me up and down, from black eyeglasses to red hightop sneakers, as if she'd never seen me before, as if knowing that I liked "bugs" made me an entirely different creature.

"Wow," she said.

The way she said that "wow" made me think that something had just happened, something important. But I didn't know what.

She took the ends of some of her hairs between her fingers, rolled them between thumb and index finger, and then absentmindedly placed the hairs into her mouth and started biting them.

I'd never seen someone chew on her hair before.

Then she spat it out. "You know," she said, and she looked out over the pond, "some people — and I'm not saying this because I want to call you a name, but I think you ought to know — some people call you a geek."

Her friends, I thought. Her giggly friends call me a geek. I gazed at the water, like her. I think at this point we felt it was easier to talk if we didn't actually look at each other. Some mallard ducks came swimming toward us from the middle of the pond.

"But they're wrong," she said. "You're not a geek. Although you *are* . . ."

"What?"

"Different. I mean . . . you're the only kid in school who — you're the only kid I've ever heard of — maybe you're the only kid in the *world* — who has only one name. How come you don't have a first name?"

So I explained, as I always have to. My parents left the first name blank on my birth certificate because they had this idea — a goofy idea, they now admit — that I should choose my own name. Meanwhile, they called me Baby. And then Baba, because that's what I started saying. And when I finally got old enough to choose, they found out it was too late to change the birth certificate.

"But," Kirsten said, "people could *call* you a different name even if it isn't on your birth certificate."

"Yes. But I don't want them to."

"Because you want to be different."

"Because I want to be . . . who I am."

She furrowed her dark eyebrows. "You are definitely Babcock," she said. "Babcock and his briefcase."

"It comes in handy."

"Did you bring it here?"

I pointed to it leaning against the trunk of a willow tree.

"What's in that briefcase, anyway?"

I didn't answer. What I did do, though, was move my lips and hold out my hand. *Dragonfly, dragonfly, come to me before I die.*

Soon, one came. Kirsten didn't move. She watched in silence as it perched on my fingertip and then flew away. With her eyes still focused on the disappearing dragonfly, she said something that caught me by surprise. She asked, "Are you gifted?"

I shrugged.

She was looking at me now. She said, "I know your grades are better than mine."

"How do you know?"

"Come *on.* Everybody knows."

Nothing is secret in this town.

"And," she said, "I see you reading *books* all the time."

"So?"

"That's what *gifted* people do." She cleared her throat. I think she realized that what she'd said sounded a little strange. "Actually," she continued, "my mother says that everyone is gifted in their own way." She cleared her throat again. "And whatever my special gift is, it isn't getting A's."

"Maybe it's gymnastics," I said.

"No. It isn't." She threw a pebble in the water. "I'm sorry I killed your bug. I'm sorry I called you fat."

"I *am* fat."

She stood up. "And I *am* flat," she said. "But I'm still hoping something will happen."

"It probably will," I said. "Maybe in a big way. Maybe it will be your special gift."

She looked startled.

I can't quite believe I said that. I felt myself blushing, though I don't think she saw it. Of course, it's hard to tell when I blush.

She stared at me for a moment. And then . . . I saw it.

She smiled.

A smile that was all freckles and ears. She turned one last handspring. And she ran away. She ran with grace. She ran like a breeze slipping over the grass.

THE JUVENILE REPTILE

We had this band. We practiced in my garage. My father parked his MG outside when we wanted to play.

Dylan was playing keyboards. He was in his third year of lessons. I played guitar — second year. Boone played bass guitar with no lessons at all. We sounded about like you'd expect: You could recognize the song if you already knew it. We also had a drummer by the name of Law. He was good. The trouble was, drums can't carry the melody.

Starting a band was my idea. The name I gave it was Two One Five Five Two. Boone said we should be called The Four Hairs because we each looked so different. Boone had brown hair that was all cowlick: It would lie down if he wetted it, but when it dried it just stood straight up like a hedgehog. So he kept it short. Law had blond hair, casual and shaggy — the surfer look. Dylan had sleek black hair. Dylan's a sharp dresser — black turtlenecks, leather shoes. He wears an earring. He carries a comb in his back pocket and always keeps every last hair in place. My hair is curly, medium length.

We didn't perform for anybody — we knew our limits — but we had fun messing around in my garage. I did most of the singing. Boone would back me up sometimes, but he couldn't harmonize. Dylan could harmonize, but he didn't have much of a voice. Law flat out refused to sing.

We argued about what we should play and how we should sound. Boone wanted us to be Jan and Dean: white bread. I wanted to do rap or sing oldies like B. B. King: dark pumpernickel. So Dylan got us to compromise on whole wheat: Chuck Berry and a bit of Bo Diddley. We butchered them. Sometimes we tried to play new songs that we copied off the radio, but we were more comfortable with oldies. The only one who didn't care what we played was Law: He could tap out a beat for anything.

Then one day we decided to write a song. Dylan suggested it. We'd made up raps before. They were easy. Dylan, though, was talking about something new for us. He was talking about *music*. He was probably the only member of the band with any real musical talent — that is, not counting Law's sense of rhythm. Dylan liked to make up little tunes on the keyboard — not whole songs, just little bits of tune.

Law tapped out a beat on the drums. Law's family is rich, but we don't hold that against him. Actually, his mother's a real nice lady. His father is a jerk. Law's just like a regular kid, mostly, except he goes to a private school and he has two sets of drums: a new set at home and an old set that he leaves in the corner of my garage for the band. And though he looks it, he's never surfed. *Bum bum bum, bum-bump a dumpa dumpa.* "How's that for a beat?" Law asked.

"I can dance to it," Dylan said. "Now we need a tune."

"And words," I said.

"I'll do the tune," Dylan said. "You do the words." He started fooling around on the keyboard.

Bum bum bum, bum bump a dumpa dumpa. Bum bum bum, bum-bump a dumpa dumpa.

I listened to the drums, and — to my surprise — I already knew the words. "I've got it," I said. "Listen: 'Dragonfly, Dragonfly, are you friendly? Are you shy?'"

"What's that man?" Boone asked.

"It sucks," Law said.

"We don't want to write a song about *insects*," Dylan said. "We want a song about people. About *song* stuff. You know. About *sex*. About *drugs*. About rock and *roll*."

"At least," Boone said, "it has to be about people."

"Maybe it is about people," I said. The thought had just occurred to me.

"You mean 'Dragonfly' is a nickname?" Boone asked.

"It could be," I said.

"Boy or girl?" Boone asked.

"Girl," I said. Though until that moment, I hadn't thought about it.

"Now it makes sense," Boone said. "'Dragonfly, Dragonfly, are you friendly? Are you shy?' I like it."

"Go with it," Law said.

Bum bum bum, bum-bump a dumpa dumpa.

I went with it. I grabbed a pencil and paper and started writing down words. Law kept drumming. Dylan tried out notes on the keyboard. Boone told him what he liked and what he didn't.

I was surprised at how easily the words came. Of course I had to cross things out and draw arrows to move lines around, but pretty quickly I came up with something. I read it aloud:

Dragonfly, Dragonfly,
Are you friendly? Are you shy?
You turn cartwheels on my shoes,
Make me lose these muddy blues.

Wild as the starry sky,
Eyes like lapis lazuli,
A thousand freckles, two big ears,
You don't need no big brassiere.

"Hey," Law said. "You can't say 'brassiere.'"

"Why not?" I said. "I've heard worse. Listen to the radio."

"I don't mean they won't let you say it. I mean it's *stupid.*"

"All right," I said. "How about: 'A thousand freckles, two big ears, stay with me a hundred years'?"

"Yes," Law said.

"So you like it?" I asked.

"No," Boone said. "What do you mean about lapis lazuli?"

"It's a kind of rock," I said. "I mean her eyes are blue like lapis lazuli."

"Her eyes are like rocks?" Boone said. "That's not . . . pretty."

"Lapis lazuli is a pretty rock," I said.

"It sucks," Law said.

"Well then, how about this? 'Wild as the starry sky, golden hair except the eye.'"

"What does that mean?" Boone asked. "You don't have hair on your eyeballs."

"I mean she has blonde hair except her eyebrows are dark."

"Maybe that's what you mean," Boone said, "but it isn't what it says."

"It sucks," Law said. "Anyway, if her hair is blonde, then her eyebrows are blonde. Like mine."

"Not her," I said.

"Who?" Law asked.

"Nobody," I said. "It's just a song."

"Then give her black hair," Law said. "'Black of hair and blue of eye.' How's that?"

"Good," Boone said.

"No," I said. "She's blonde."

"Babcock. It's only a song."

"She's *blonde*."

"All right, all right," Law said. "'Blonde of hair and blue of eye.' Is that what you want?"

"Yes."

"Do dragonflies have hair?" Boone asked.

"Yes," I said.

Dylan had worked out a simple tune. He told me what chords to play on the guitar, and then he showed Boone how to play the simple bass line — there were only about four notes. Meanwhile, I made up another verse. We ran through it a couple of times, trying to get synchronized. And Danny showed up.

Danny was the Fifth Hair: black, thick, un-combed, wild. He had no interest in playing in a band and probably couldn't sit still long enough to learn an instrument, anyway, but he liked to check on what we were doing. As Law was rich, Danny was poor. My father once said, "Danny was born poor and raised poorly." His mother came from Mexico and died when he was a baby. His father let him run wild — or run free, depending on how you looked at it. Danny had an amazing bicycle that he put together out of junk parts, including some pedals that he got from me. The front wheel was smaller than the rear. He said he built it that way so he could always go downhill. The brakes squeaked like fingernails on a blackboard. Danny was a builder. A freeloader. And a friend.

We played our new song. I included the new verse:

I'm a reptile, juvenile,
Make me human with your smile.

When we finished, Danny looked puzzled. "It's a song about a reptile? And he's in love with an insect?"

"He *feels* like a reptile," I explained. "But she makes him feel human."

"And she's a dragonfly?"

"It's a nickname."

"Who is she?"

"Nobody."

"I want to meet her," Danny said. "I feel like a reptile all the time."

"Right," Dylan said. "You look like one, too." Dylan and Danny aren't exactly friends.

Danny ignored him. He said, "I want to meet her. You say she's skinny. Like me."

It's true that Danny is the thinnest boy in San Puerco. But I said, "It's just a song, Danny. Anyway, she wouldn't like you."

"How do you know?" Danny asked. "If it's just a song, why couldn't she like me?"

"Because I wrote the words. And I know she wouldn't like you." I felt my lip starting to twitch. So I smiled.

"I don't remember hearing some line saying 'She doesn't like Danny.' Maybe you wrote it, but I *heard* it. And I can hear whatever I want in a song. Why wouldn't she like me, Babcock?"

"Because," I said, "here's the next verse:

Tell your nanny, tell your granny,
You don't like the boy named Danny."

"What is this?" Danny asked. "Is she your girlfriend or something?"

"Don't be silly," I said.

We liked our new song so much, talking it over at school next day, we decided we were ready to play for an audience. We'd have an open house — that is, an open garage. Law designed a poster on his computer and printed a few dozen copies:

OPEN GARAGE!
SEE THE HOT NEW BAND
TWO ONE FIVE FIVE TWO!
REFRESHMENTS.
FREE ADMISSION.

We stapled the posters to telephone poles around town. And while eating dinner, I happened to mention the plan to my parents.

"You're going to *what?*"

"In our *garage?*"

They seemed to have the idea that the band would attract motorcycle gangs, drunks, drug addicts, people who punch out windows and spray graffiti on walls — in other words, the kind of people who went to the kind of dances *they* used to go to.

I told them we'd be lucky to get a few kids from my seventh-grade class, if anybody. The refreshments would be some two-liter bottles of soda pop. The town was too small to have a motorcycle gang, and no drunks or druggies were going to come drink orange soda and watch some thirteen-year-old boys play in a garage.

"At least, for a rock and roll band, you seem to have a nice sense of humility," my father chuckled.

"Now, Thomas, don't get upset," my mother said, looking upset. "Don't have a heart attack."

"Do I look upset?" my father asked, leaning back in his chair and lighting his pipe.

My mother is always afraid that my father is going to have a heart attack — like her father and her grandfather. My father's never had any trouble; he gets checkups every year, and the doctor always tells him that his only problem is that he's overweight — which he is. And the reason he's overweight is that my mother is such a great cook.

"You might as well use the garage now while you still can," my father said. "Pretty soon, I'm going to convert it into a studio."

"Thomas," my mother said, "you know we can't afford —"

"*When* we can afford it," he added.

That satisfied my mother. She knew we'd never be able to pay for it. My father runs a car repair shop. In the evenings at home, he likes to draw. He's been playing around with different ideas for comic strips, which he tries to sell to newspapers. Nobody has ever bought one. The drawing is good, but I think the ideas are dumb — like a superhero dog who can fly. He says if he ever gets the comic strip going, he'll quit the car repair business, build a studio in the garage, and get paid for doing what he loves: drawing.

The other thing he loves doing is taking care of his old MG. If he didn't already run a repair shop, I think he'd have to buy one just so he could keep that MG running. It's an antique. It's always breaking down. But he waxes it every weekend, takes it to car shows, and belongs to an MG club. My mother says it's the only MG in the world that comes equipped with a matching sofa and loveseat, automatic dishwasher, and membership in a health club — because whenever she's suggested buying those things, my father has always said he needed the money to fix some piece of the car.

My mother understands money. She's more practical than my father. She's a bookkeeper, so she keeps track of money all day. I used to think a bookkeeper was like a librarian, but then my mother explained that instead of putting books onto shelves she was putting numbers into columns. She said that her job did have one thing in common with being a librarian: She had to separate the fiction from the nonfiction.

"So we can do it?" I asked.

My father took the pipe from his lips, blew a puff of smoke, and said, "You'll have to let us chaperone, son."

"But — please — don't be too *obvious,* okay?"

My father chuckled. "We'll try not to embarrass you, son. We'll just try to blend in with the crowd."

"You *can't* blend in. Oh my God! You won't try to *dance,* will you?"

My father met my mother's eye. They both were grinning.

I said, "Are you going to *humiliate* me?"

"Don't worry," my mother said. "Just play some nice waltzes. And something we can Charleston to."

"And maybe we can do a minuet," my father added.

"You *are* kidding, aren't you?"

They didn't answer. They just grinned.

SOW BUGS

Outside school I was standing with Danny and Boone, waiting until the last minute to go inside. Out of the corner of my eye, I saw three girls walking toward us. Whispering. Giggling.

I set down my briefcase. I raised my hands above my head.

Boone looked at me. "What are you doing?" he said.

I leaned to the side, kicked off with my feet — and fell on my back. My eyeglasses fell off my face and skidded across the concrete.

"What was *that?*" Danny asked.

"Cartwheel," I said, reaching for my glasses and putting them on. One of the lenses was scratched. The three girls were walking away. Giggling. One was skinny. Blonde hair. Big ears.

At lunch I was walking to join Danny and Boone when Kirsten came toward me and without a word handed me a cube of paper and then walked away. It was regular notebook paper, folded and taped. It rattled. I peeled the tape and unfolded one end.

Inside was a green grasshopper.

Quick as a flash before I could reclose the paper, it hopped out of the cube and onto my ear and just as quickly hopped again from my ear and away.

I looked around.

Kirsten was gone.

The grasshopper was gone.

All that remained was a slight tingling on my ear and a cube of notebook paper in my hand.

After school I was walking up the street to my house, watching clouds, and I didn't notice until I almost tripped over it: a dead possum. A car had run over it. The body had split, and guts were spilling out.

I hate cars.

I walked up the street wondering how we could train all the wild animals in the world to stay out of the road — or how we could give them weapons to fight back. Just as a skunk has its smelly spray, just as a porcupine has its quills, maybe animals could develop weapons against cars. Nails, maybe, that could pop the tires. Sugar water that they could squirt in the gas tank.

As I was thinking these thoughts, gradually I was becoming aware that the road was alive. That is, the asphalt was dead as always but crawling over it were dozens — no hundreds — probably *thousands* — of little gray sow bugs. Now, of course, there are always sow bugs in San Puerco. You see them if you turn over a log or pick up a brick. But this was different. This was a sow bug *party*. I leaned down for a closer look. Where were they going? And why? They cruised along like busy little limousines. Some headed left, some headed right, some wandered up the road, some down. If I touched one, it would curl into a ball.

I held a finger down to the road. A sow bug

stopped, tested the fingertip with its little antennae, and then it started climbing over my fingernail, over my knuckle into a forest of hair, tickling with its tiny feet. It looked like a miniature armadillo.

I heard a car coming. Not just coming — it was roaring and squealing up our winding street. I couldn't see it because I was at a curve. I stood up with the sow bug still on my finger. I stayed right in the middle of the road.

My lip had started to twitch.

I heard the car roaring — too fast — closer and closer, and I heard the tires squeal as they started to take the corner. Then I saw it. The car was swaying to the side with the tires just barely holding onto the asphalt as the driver leaned into the steering wheel. And he saw me: standing, blocking the middle of the street. He had no time to stop. He hit the horn and threw the steering wheel around — and I jumped just out of the way, fell down and rolled over twice — as he crashed into the ditch at the side of the road with a screech of brake and a crunch of metal.

Then there was silence.

But only for a moment. The driver threw open his door and jumped out of the car. He was a tall, skinny black man with a stubby mustache. "Did I hit you?" he said.

"No, sir," I said, standing up. The sow bug was gone from my finger. I guess it jumped, too. "I dodged, sir."

"Damn," he said. "I should've hit you."

"What, sir?"

"You deserved it. What were you doing standing — smiling! — in the middle of the road? Didn't you hear me coming? Look at this car! Look at this fender!"

I was looking. It was an old green Cadillac Coupe De Ville with rust under the doors and a coat hanger for an antenna. The tires were bald. The backseat was loaded with scruffy old suitcases and cardboard boxes tied up with twine.

"I asked you a question, boy. Didn't you hear me coming?"

"Yes, sir."

"Then why didn't you move?"

"I didn't think you'd take a blind curve on a one-lane road at forty miles an hour."

"And *I* didn't think you'd be standing in the middle of the road. And what *were* you doing there?"

"I wanted you to stop."

"You *wanted* me to stop. Why did you *want* me to stop?"

"The sow bugs, sir."

"The *what?*"

"Sow bugs. Sir. I didn't want you to run over the —"

"You made me wreck my car because of a damn *insect?*"

"Thousands of them, sir. Actually, they aren't insects. They're crustaceans. They're related to —"

"I don't believe it."

"— crabs."

"What?"

"Crabs, sir. Sow bugs are related to crabs."

"I'll crab *you,* boy. Now get over here and help push this car out of this ditch."

"Sir, I think you'd better walk. Leave the car here. You can get it later. I'll help you. The sow bugs are still all over the road."

The man glared at me with his hands on his hips. "Do you *hear* me?" he said. "Are we speaking the same *language?*"

"Yes, sir."

"What is your *attitude,* boy?"

"My attitude?"

"Never *mind*." He threw his hands up in the air. "I'll do it myself. And if you're still in this road when I come through, you're gonna be one big, fat, *dead* sow bug cuz I ain't gonna stop. I ain't even gonna slow *down*. In fact, next time I see you in the road I'm gonna go *faster*."

With that, he stepped into the Cadillac and slammed the door. He tried to back up. The rear wheels spun. He gunned the engine. The wheels spun faster, and smoke rose into the air. He punched his open hand against the steering wheel. And then, while he wasn't giving it any gas, the car started to back out. He'd been trying too hard.

Once he was back in the road, he looked at me and scowled. I didn't try to stand in his way. Suddenly with a roar and a spinning of wheels, he started fishtailing up the narrow street. In a moment he was gone, leaving the smoke and the smell of burnt rubber.

Behind him, on the asphalt, I found hundreds of little gray bodies — crushed. They hadn't even had time to roll up in a ball.

PEANUT BUTTER AND SAUERKRAUT

When I came to my house, the Cadillac was parked in my driveway next to my mother's van. Right away my lip started to twitch.

My mother was out in the driveway next to the Coupe De Ville. She gave the man a big hug, slapping her hands on his back. Then she stepped back from him and saw me coming.

"Baba!" she called. "Come meet your Uncle Earl."

Uncle Earl saw me, and he looked startled. Then he smiled. "We've already met," he said. "I — uh — I ran into him, just down the road. That is, I *almost* ran into him."

Mother smiled. "That's nice," she said. "But Earl, why didn't you tell us you were coming?"

"Oh, I just thought I'd come by and give you a holler."

"But can you stay a while?"

"Oh, I reckon, if it ain't too much trouble."

"No trouble at all. We'd love to have you stay."

Where? We didn't have a spare room. But I didn't have to wonder for long.

"We'll put you in Baba's room."

"Baba?" Uncle Earl said. "You call him Baba?"

"Well, you know, Earl, he was supposed to choose his own name. Only he never did. So we had to call him something. Baba is what he used to say, before he could say Babcock. And of course we can't call him *that*, because it's our name, too."

"So," Uncle Earl said, looking down at me, "you want me to call you Baba, too?"

"No, sir," I said.

"What should I call you?"

"My friends call me Babcock."

"Like your mama say, I can't call you *that*."

"One of my friends calls me Badger."

"Not bad," Uncle Earl said, fingering his mustache. "But based on what I know about you, based on what I seen, I think I got a better name for you: Beauregard. Beauregard Bodacious Babcock. How does that strike you?"

"Terrible, sir."

"Beau, for short. Or Beau Bo. I like the ring of that. Beau Bo Babcock. Hee-hee!" Uncle Earl slapped his leg.

I turned to my mother. "How long is he staying?"

My mother frowned. I knew it was a rude question. "As long as he wants," she said. She looked at me sharply. "Uncle Earl is family. And family is always welcome at our house."

Uncle Earl looked at me with what I thought was a smirk.

My father's MG drove into the driveway and parked behind the Cadillac. More squashed sow bugs, I thought. My father stepped out and broke into a grin. He walked up and shook Uncle Earl's hand. "Earl!" he said. "Nice to see you. What kind of trouble are you in now?"

"Thomas," Mother said. "Don't tease my brother."

"I'm not teasing," Father said, still smiling.

"I'm just asking. If you're visiting us, I know you're on the lam from something. What is it this time — money? Or women?"

"I'm just taking a little vacation," Uncle Earl said, and I noticed that his upper lip had started to twitch.

I guess it runs in the family.

My mother cooked up a storm that night.

I stared at the slice of pork on my plate, that slice of flesh that once had been part of a living, breathing animal, and then I stared at the gravy dribbling off the biscuits with bits of meat and grease — guts spilling out of a run-over possum. I poked my fork into the green beans with little bits of bacon mixed in — sow bugs squashed into the road.

I pushed the plate aside.

My mother asked, "What's the matter, Baba? Aren't you feeling well?"

"I feel fine. I've just made up my mind."

"About what, son?"

"I'm a vegetarian."

"Oh, no, Baba, you don't want to be a vegetarian. Vegetarians don't eat right. It isn't natural. They don't get enough protein. The only way to get enough protein if you're a vegetarian is to eat all those beans and things, and then you'll get fat."

"I am fat."

"Don't you like my cooking?"

"I love your cooking. That's why I'm fat."

"Do you want to lose weight? We could put you on a diet. You don't have to be a vegetarian if you want to lose —"

"No, ma'am. I don't want to lose weight."

"Then why do you want to be a vegetarian?"

"Because I hate cars."

My father froze with his water glass halfway to his mouth. He stared at me. He said, "You hate cars? What does that have to do with being a vegetarian? We aren't eating cars here, are we? And what does that say about me? Do you hate me, too, because I work on cars?"

"No sir, I don't hate you. It has nothing to do with you. And nothing to do with cars. The thing is —"

"You just said you were a vegetarian because you hate cars. Now you say it has nothing to do with —"

"Cars kill animals. I like animals. I don't want to eat animals. That's all I meant."

My mother laid a hand on my arm. She said, "If you become a vegetarian, Baba, do you expect us to become vegetarians, too? Do you expect your Uncle Earl to become a vegetarian?"

"No, ma'am."

"Then do you expect me to cook a separate meal just for you?"

"No, ma'am." I pushed my chair away from the table.

"Where are you going?"

"To the kitchen. To make a sandwich."

"I don't think we have anything. Except sauerkraut."

She knew I hated sauerkraut. I said, "Do we have any peanut butter?"

"Yes."

"Good. I'll make a peanut butter and sauerkraut sandwich."

As I walked into the kitchen, I heard my father say, "Don't worry. This too shall pass."

I brought the sandwich back to the table and ate it, every last crumb of it. Then I licked my lips, just to show them I was happy. I drank a glass of milk. I still could taste sauerkraut in my mouth. I looked at my plate. It didn't look like possum guts any more, or even like sow bugs. It looked like food. I was still hungry. But there's one thing about me that's stronger than hunger: I'm stubborn.

"Mmm-mmm. This sure is fine pork roast," Uncle Earl said. He looked at my mother and winked.

"Wonderful gravy," my father said. "And I just love bacon with my green beans."

"May I be excused?" I said.

"Wait until dinner is over," Mother said.

And I knew they could be just as strong-minded as me. I guess *that* runs in the family, too.

"Yes," Uncle Earl said. "Wait and watch us eat some *real* food."

"Is there dessert?" I said.

"Yes," my mother said. "Your favorite. Apple pie."

Uncle Earl got a twinkle in his eye. An *evil*-looking twinkle, if you ask me. He said, "Would there just happen to be any lard in that pie crust?"

"I wasn't going to mention it," my mother said. "But yes, there is."

"And isn't lard made out of animal fat?" Uncle Earl said.

"Yes," my mother said.

Uncle Earl turned to me. "And how do you feel about eating animal fat, Mr. Vegee-terar-ian?"

"May I be excused?" I said.

"No," my father said.

"It looks like there's going to be an extra piece of apple pie for us to share," Uncle Earl said. "Mmm-mmm. Is it that delicious Dutch crumb apple pie just like Mama used to make?"

"Yes," my mother said. She frowned. She likes it when I enjoy her cooking.

"I just *love* Dutch crumb apple pie," Uncle Earl said, looking at me. "I'm sure glad there'll be an *extra* piece."

"May I *please* be excused?"

"No," my father said.

"Yes," my mother said, glaring at Uncle Earl.

I left the table and went to my room — or what used to be my room. Uncle Earl had piled his raggedy suitcases and boxes wrapped with twine on the bed, the mouse cage, the terrariums, even on the fish tank. I moved a box and opened the lid to the aquarium and fed my two goldfish named Sojourner and Truth. In a peanut butter jar next to them, a dozen tadpoles wiggled in circles. Next, in a mayonnaise jar a bunch of dragonfly larvae rested under a stalk of duckweed. On the windowsill lay a few chrysalids from which butterflies soon would emerge. I peeked in the terrarium where Marcus, the horned toad, squatted on a rock while Garvey, the blue-bellied lizard, did push-ups in one corner. Martin Luther, the kingsnake, stared hungrily at them from his own terrarium next door. Martin Luther had a permanent smile fixed on his face — probably the same smile that I got when I was angry.

I unrolled my sleeping bag and lay down on the floor. It was too early to go to bed, but I wanted to be alone. I wanted to think. I heard the mice, Frederick and Douglass, scurrying in their wood shavings. I heard the hum of the motor pumping air to Sojourner and Truth. I heard nothing from Marcus, the horned toad. He *never* moved. Sometimes I worried that Marcus would die and I wouldn't even know it until he started to rot. In the darkness, in silence, Martin Luther slithered; the tadpoles swam; the dragonfly larvae oozed along. Inside the chrysalids, invisible, in silence, caterpillars were working miracles.

Lately I've felt like a chrysalid myself. And I wonder, when I crack my cocoon, what strange winged beast will crawl into the light of day?

THE REAL WORLD

I had just drifted off to sleep when Uncle Earl came into the room, switching on the light, slamming the door, humming to himself. He was not the quiet type. I tried to roll over and cover my head, but Uncle Earl said, "Hey. What's with this place, anyway?"

"What do you mean, sir?"

"I thought you guys lived in California."

"We do, sir."

"That's what my map say, too. But that road is West Virginia. These mountains are West Virginia. I had to stop three times and eee-*gur*-gitate."

"What, sir?"

"E*gur*gitate. Unswallow."

"You were carsick, sir?"

"I didn't say I was carsick. I just say I had to e*gur*gitate a few times. I never thought my own sister would live in a place that would make me *puke.* I thought she lived near San Francisco. It *looks* near, on the map."

"It's a couple hours driving."

"A couple hours e*gur*gitating, you mean. This is just a teenie *weenie* town. You could put both City Limit signs on the same *post.* You can't even get a *drink* in this town."

"Yes you can, sir. There's a Coke machine at the bait shop."

"What bait shop?"

"Outside town. There's a shack by the road. You'll see a sign out front. It says WORM FARM."

"I'm talking about getting a *drink* and you're telling me to go to some place called the *Worm Farm?*"

"You can go to the restaurant."

"I saw that itty bitty restaurant. It's so small, the flies have to wait in line for a table." He imitated a hostess's voice: "Bluebottle fly. Party of four. Your table is now ready. Fruit fly. Party of six hundred. Your garbage can is now ready."

"You can go to the bar."

"What bar? Where?"

So I told him where the tavern was located. And after that, Uncle Earl seemed to have run out of things to say. In a minute, he was asleep with a rattling snore like grinding gears.

I woke up in my sleeping bag on the floor in the middle of the night. Uncle Earl was snorting and groaning and thrashing around on my bed. He made as much noise sleeping as when he was awake. I didn't see how he could be getting any rest. It looked as if he was having a wrestling match with his sheet. Suddenly he rolled over and made a sound as if he was blowing his nose into the pillow. Then he lay quietly.

Another sound came faintly from another part of the house: the rustle of paper. The scratching of a pencil.

I got up and walked to the kitchen. My father had a drawing board set up on the table. His back was to me. I watched from the doorway, and he didn't know I was there. The clock on the wall said 2:14 A.M. He'd drawn four squares for a comic strip, and now he was filling it in.

First he made bubbles of dialogue. Then he drew a knight in armor and a woman on a castle turret, and then a dragon.

I wished he could sell his comic strip to the newspapers for a million dollars. I wished he didn't have to stay up late and lose sleep and then feel tired all day while he was repairing cars. I wished he had a drawing studio instead of having to work on the kitchen table, having to wait until all the meals were served and the food was cleared.

My father sat back in his chair and relit his pipe.

"Is it done?"

He jumped at the sound of my voice. Then he smiled. "Done for tonight," he said.

"Could I see it?"

He gestured for me to take a look.

I read it.

"You didn't laugh," my father said.

I looked at him. "It isn't funny," I said.

Suddenly my father slashed a big X across the page.

"Is that better?" he asked.

"No."

He put his head in his hands, tired and sad.

"I'm sorry," I said.

"So am I," he said through his hands. Then he sat back and put the pipe to his mouth.

"Is this fun?" I asked. "Is this what you really want to do?"

"Yes."

"Why?"

"Because," he said, holding the pipe in his hand, "if I don't repair somebody's car, some other mechanic will do it. But if I don't draw my cartoons, *nobody* else can do it. Only I know what I want to say."

He stared into the bowl of his pipe.

"What do you want to say?" I asked.

"That's the problem. I don't know, exactly."

I wanted to make him feel better. I said, "Somebody was just telling me that we each have a special gift. I guess drawing is your gift."

"I hope so, son. I hope so."

"Why don't you draw something *real?* Instead of knights and castles or superhero dogs. Draw the real world."

My father wrinkled his nose. He tapped his pipe. He said, "The real world isn't very funny, son. Sometimes the real world is an awful place. We protect you from it. There's no problems in this town. That's why I like it here."

He was wrong. San Puerco has certain peo-
ple, certain ignorant people. *Hey nigger.* I hear it.
Anyway, he doesn't live here just to protect me.
He also lives here because of the price of
houses. They cost less in San Puerco because
there aren't any jobs. You have to drive an hour
to get to Pulgas Park, where my father's garage
is.

"I'm not as protected as you think," I said.

"You think you know the real world?" My father waved his pipe toward the bedroom. "You
could ask your Uncle Earl. He's seen the real
world. He's seen a lot of it."

I'd heard some stories about Uncle Earl. I'd
heard he was arrested for speeding in Missis-
sippi and spent thirty days in jail. I'd heard bits
of other stories, but my mother always stopped
talking about them when she saw that I was listening.

"He's scared of the mountains," I said.
"Scared of the roads. But he drives way too fast.
And then he gets carsick."

"Earl's a city boy," my father said. "He's always lived in cities."

"He sleeps funny. He makes noise. He throws
himself around on the bed."

"Maybe that's the real world, coming back to him," my father said.

Back in bed, I lay awake. I was thinking about the real world. I know real. One night my mother was driving me home in the van on the highway that twists down the mountain through the redwood forests to our town, and we were talking and playing the radio and feeling relaxed — when a pair of headlights swung around a corner and headed straight at us. My mother made a hissing sound through her teeth as she cut hard on the steering wheel. A split second later, the headlights crunched into the side of the van and caromed off again. I was thrown against the door in my seat belt, and my mother jerked toward my seat in hers. We were stopped. The other headlights were stopped. My mother looked at me wildly and shouted, "Are you all right?"

"Yes." My shoulder felt bruised. "Are you?"

"Yes."

Just then we heard the screech of tires, and the headlight — just one, now — took off up the road.

"Get him!" I shouted. "Follow him! It's a hit-and-run. He's getting away!"

My mother opened the door and stared up the highway as the taillights disappeared. She looked down at the deep ugly gash in the side of the van. There were no houses nearby, no other cars. Just us and giant redwood trees under silent stars. "I'm going home," she said.

"But he *hit* you. He'll get away!"

"You want me to chase a drunk up the mountain in this old van?"

"His car must be damaged, too. Maybe you can catch up."

"I'm going home."

And she drove to our house, and she threw her arms around my father, and she cried and cried. He called the sheriff, but it was too late. We didn't even know what the other car looked like except that it had one headlight. By the time my father called, it could have been anywhere.

That's the real world: two headlights coming at you in the night. And there's no time to get out of the way.

But when the real world tries to hit me and run, I'll follow. I'll chase it down and make it pay.

ABSQUATULATION

After school as I was walking home I saw Kirsten running ahead of me wearing a bright blue backpack. When she came to a telephone pole where we had stapled one of our posters about the Open Garage, she stopped and read it. I caught up with her — walking fast. I hate to run. *Hate* it.

"Are you going?" I asked.

She glanced at me, then looked back at the poster. "I can't. I'm running that day," she said. "I'm entered in a junior marathon."

"So — you like running?" I asked. Which, I knew, was a stupid question.

"I love it."

We have something in common, I thought. We both have strong feelings about running.

"I wish I could go," she said. "Nothing ever happens in this stupid town, and now when something finally does, I'll be at a marathon. But — then — my mother wouldn't let me go to a dance." She said all this while still looking at the poster, which she must have read fifty times by now.

"Why not?" I asked.

Kirsten turned to look at me. "Because she's my mother."

"What does that mean?"

"I don't know how to explain my mother."

"Give me a hint."

"Well . . ."

"What?"

"She likes palm trees."

Without another word, Kirsten started running down the street. I watched until she disappeared around a corner, ponytail bouncing on her backpack.

I knew where she lived. If her mother liked palm trees, I knew exactly where her house was. San Puerco is on the side of a mountain in the middle of a redwood forest where it's cool and shady even in the summer. There's one lot, though, where all the trees have been cleared and the sun bakes down. In front of the house there's a silver Buick station wagon and three palm trees curling upward toward the sun.

That was where Kirsten slept, where she ate her meals and did her homework: the house of the three palms. And it did give me a hint about her mother. A warning, actually. A warning that I ignored.

When I got home, my father's MG and my mother's van weren't there. He was repairing somebody's car; she was doing somebody's bookkeeping. But I wasn't alone. There was a green Cadillac with a crumpled fender.

"Hey. Hey, Beau!"

"What, sir?"

Uncle Earl was lying on my bed, smoking a Kool. The whole room smelled like tobacco smoke. I hoped it didn't bother Martin Luther or Frederick or Douglass or any member of my little zoo. Uncle Earl put down his newspaper — opened to the racing page — and said, "What's happening, bro?"

"Nothing, sir."

"Sir? I call you bro and you call me *sir?*"

"Yes, sir."

"Don't you know how to *talk?* Don't you want to sound like a brother?"

"You're not my brother."

"I'm *a* brother."

"I don't talk that way."

"You talk like your *parents.*"

"Yes, sir."

Uncle Earl was staring at me over the smoke of his cigarette. After a moment, he said, "You know what the trouble with you is, Beau? You're too *middle-class.* You and your papa, and your mama, too."

"What do you mean, sir?"

"I mean I ask you for ice cream, and you hand me something that looks like a double-scoop chocolate, but it tastes like vanilla."

"Look again, sir."

"Look at what?"

"Your cone, sir. What I give you."

"What is it?"

"Rainbow sherbet."

Uncle Earl shook his head. "Only wusses eat sherbet." He stubbed out the cigarette in a seashell of mine that he was using for an ashtray. "But I forgive you. Y'all is family, and I love you anyway."

It always surprises me how easily some people can use those words: I love you. The L-word. I'm not even sure what it *means,* exactly — scientifically. What is love? How do you explain it on the molecular level?

Uncle Earl sat up on the bed, stomped his feet on the floor, clapped his hands, and said, "You want to play some catch?"

"With what?"

"With a *baseball,* of course. You got a mitt?"

"No, sir."

"Just a minute. I got a mitt you can borrow." He opened one of his cardboard boxes and started rooting around.

I stepped outside. The air tasted clean. My father's pipe smoke didn't bother me nearly as much as the smoke of a cigarette. Law and Boone walked up the driveway. Uncle Earl was still inside. Before he could find a mitt, I went to the garage.

We didn't rehearse. I swept the floor, put my father's tools away and stacked up some buckets of paint. Boone tried to clean some oil stains on the floor while Dylan stabbed a broom at some dusty old cobwebs. Law hung two clip lights to some rafters to brighten up the corner where we were going to play.

"It still looks like a garage," I said.

"It's supposed to," Dylan said. "We're a garage band, aren't we?"

I came back to the house just before dinner.

"Where were you?" Uncle Earl said. "I found you a mitt, went out in the yard — and you'd already absquatulated."

"Ab-what?"

"Absquatulated. Gone. Vamoosed. Like a coo-ool breeze."

When I sat down for dinner, my mother gave me a guilty look and said, "It's chicken, Baba. I'm sorry. I'd already bought it before you decided to be a vegetarian."

"It's all right," I said. "I'll have peas."

Uncle Earl loaded his plate with chicken, saying, "Mmm-mmm. I sure do love fried chicken. You bread it just *right*, sister dear. I sure am glad I don't have to vegetate."

"Speaking of vegetating," my father said, "just what are you doing now, Earl? Are you looking for a job?"

Uncle Earl shifted slightly in his seat. His lip twitched — just slightly. "I'm thinking about a new career," he said.

"In what?" my father asked.

"I haven't decided."

"Can you fix cars?"

"No."

"You want to learn? You could start in my shop."

Uncle Earl shifted again in his seat. He pulled at the collar of his T-shirt as if it had suddenly gotten too tight. He said, "Where would I start?"

"You'd start by sweeping the floor and giving people rides to work after they've dropped off their cars."

"You mean I'd be a *porter?*"

"That's where you'd start. And we'd train you. Next, you'd start doing some oil changes, rotating tires, grease jobs . . ."

"Grease?" Uncle Earl curled his lip, which made his mustache stick out.

"You don't like grease, Earl?"

Uncle Earl's lip was twitching solidly now. The mustache wiggled like a fuzzy worm. He said, "I think I'm allergic to grease."

"And manual labor," my father said.

"Now, Thomas," my mother said.

"What happened to that last career you had?" my father said. "Weren't you selling used cars? In Baltimore?"

"Oh. That. Yes. Well. That was a *long* time ago. I found better opportunities than that. In Atlanta. I was in the jewelry bidness."

"The jewelry business?"

"Mostly wristwatches."

"Used wristwatches?"

"They were like new. I guaranteed them."

"What happened to that business?"

"It became time to . . . sort of . . ." Uncle Earl's lip was twitching badly.

"Absquatulate?" I suggested.

"Exactly," Uncle Earl said. "All bidness ventures run a natural cycle, and in the end you have to know when it's time to . . . absquatulate."

"What did you do after that?" my father asked.

"I had a church in Chicago."

"A church?" My mother laughed. "You?"

"I was the Reverend Earl, if you please. Founder of the Church of MegaChrist."

"And, Reverend, did that business venture run its natural cycle?" my father asked. "Or this time was the problem a woman?"

"There were some women of passionate faith," Uncle Earl said. "There was also a bit of a problem regarding the building fund." His lip twitched again. "That's why I came here."

"All the way from Chicago?" my father asked. "You *really* had to absquatulate after that one."

"Preachers don't get the respect they used to," Uncle Earl said, shaking his head. "It's a damn shame."

ROCK AND ROLL

We left the garage door open with our band set up in a corner against the back wall. We were nervous. About thirty people were standing around, spilling out of the garage, waiting for us to begin. There wasn't going to be enough soda pop. My mother was pouring it into Dixie cups. She signaled to my father that we needed more, and my father said something to Uncle Earl. It hadn't occurred to me that Uncle Earl would come, but of course he was there. I didn't have time to worry about what he might do. Danny rode up on his jalopy bicycle.

We didn't know how to begin. Dylan nudged Boone. "Say something," Dylan whispered.

Boone looked panic-stricken. "What should I say?"

"Welcome people to the garage. Tell them the soda is free. Ask them to dance if they feel like it. Introduce us. Tell them they can use the bathroom in the house. Tell them our first song will be 'Johnny B. Goode.' Say *something*."

Boone cleared his throat. "Welcome to Two One Five Hairs," he said. "The first song is in the house. I mean Johnny B. Goode is in the bathroom. I mean you can soda if you want. Say something, and we hope you like it."

Everybody stared at us. Dylan rolled his eyes. I wanted to hide. Nobody made a sound.

Suddenly Uncle Earl started clapping. A few other people clapped, and I seized the moment to start playing. A couple of beats later, the rest of the band joined in. We'd chosen to open with "Johnny B. Goode" because we knew it the best and also because we figured that even if we flubbed it, it was such a good song that it would sort of take care of itself. Instead of the Chuck Berry guitar licks, though, which I wasn't sure I could pull off on my guitar, we let Dylan carry the song with his keyboard. It was a little strange when I sang the line about playing a guitar just like ringing a bell, and then instead of a guitar twanging you heard a keyboard tweedling. But it worked. And as I sang — scared to death that I'd forget the words, or my voice would crack, or my fly was down — I looked out at the people in the garage and saw an amazing thing start to happen. They started to dance. First two kids, then a couple more, and then — oh, no! — my father and mother. They joined hands and pushed off from each other, and then my mother spun around under my father's hand, the way movies showed people dancing in the fifties. Touch dancing. And it didn't look bad, either. It must have been what Chuck Berry saw when he sang back then. Suddenly I felt part of a long tradition. I felt that Chuck Berry would approve of our little dance in our little garage. Maybe he started out the same way. All these thoughts flashed through my mind as I tried to play the right chords and sing the right words and stay in sync with the band and make sure my fly wasn't down. I don't think I'd ever worked so hard or thought so fast — except when I played soccer.

I heard a car start. It was Uncle Earl, backing out of the driveway.

I flubbed a few notes. Boone flubbed quite a few, but I don't think anybody cared. That's the nice thing about bass guitar — nobody notices it, anyway. Dylan was strong on keyboards, and Law kept a perfect beat for the people dancing. And then it was over, and people stopped dancing . . . and they clapped.

They liked it!

We all looked at each other — Law, Dylan, Boone, and me — and we grinned. What a relief. I stopped feeling so nervous. Then Dylan played a few notes on the keyboard — *plink plink plink, plink plink, plink plink plink, plink plink* — and my parents recognized them and smiled, and we plunged into "Louie Louie."

And people danced. My mother and father danced, too, but this time they weren't touching. They were shaking and bumping.

They knew more than I'd given them credit for.

Geraldine was standing right in front of the band, watching Dylan. Geraldine's my age, but she's tall. She has hair in a big curly ball like an Afro, but she's white — I think — though she's sort of dark-skinned. She's one of the best soccer players in town. She's been hanging around with Danny a lot, lately, but as we played

"Louie Louie" Danny approached her, and Geraldine shook her head, and then Danny stomped off in disgust while she kept her eyes on Dylan. I figured Danny had asked her to dance, and she'd said no. And I figured what really bothered Danny wasn't just that she wouldn't dance with him, but that she was making eyes at Dylan. You see, Dylan's always been fond of Geraldine, and Danny knows it, and that's why Dylan and Danny aren't too friendly with each other.

I was beginning to realize that a lot can happen when you bring a bunch of people together with music, and not all of it has to do with the music you're making.

Next we played a slow song, one that had just been a hit and you could still hear on the radio, and we ran into problems. First, nobody danced — except my mother and father. Second, if you flub a note on a slow song, it stands out. And after I flubbed one note, I got flustered and flubbed a few more. I thought the song would never end. Fortunately, halfway through it, Uncle Earl returned with a cardboard box full of big bottles of soda pop, and everybody went to get a drink. We skipped a verse and ended the song as quickly as we could.

Nobody clapped after that one.

We played three more fast songs, and then we took a break. I was sweating and my throat was dry. I headed straight for the drinks. A lot of people said things to me, encouraging me or congratulating me or just teasing me in a friendly sort of way, and one of them was Danny saying something about how on television he'd just seen a man set fire to the back wheel of his motorcycle and then ride it around and how cool it looked and wouldn't Geraldine be impressed if she saw something like that, which I thought was a weird thing to talk about to somebody who was in the middle of a performance. Geraldine was talking to Dylan, and Dylan was showing her something on the keyboard. And Uncle Earl — uh-oh. Uncle Earl was talking to Law. I hoped he wouldn't do something to embarrass me. I wanted to explain to Law that even though he was my uncle, I didn't *choose* him, so I shouldn't be held responsible if he did something stupid. Uncle Earl was holding the drumsticks, and as he spoke to Law he was tapping out a soft rhythm on the drums. Law looked fascinated.

I went back to the band's corner of the garage and picked up my guitar. Uncle Earl gave Law a thumbs-up and a grin, and he walked away. Law turned to me and said, "Your uncle is *cool*." Law's eyes were gleaming. "Did you know he used to play drums for Chuck Berry?"

"He did?"

We played five more songs, and our playing got more raggedy as we went on because we were doing songs that we hadn't rehearsed as much. But more people danced, the longer we kept playing. As long as Law kept the beat steady, they could dance. We played better on the old songs than the newer ones. Maybe we should be an oldies band — except for our own new material.

Uh-oh. Uncle Earl, holding a big floppy straw hat, was going from one person to the next, shaking the hat in front of their faces, and the people were dropping money into it. We'd advertised this as a free event. Was he planning to keep the money for himself? From the way my father talked about Uncle Earl, I didn't know what to expect.

We closed out with "Dragonfly." But we didn't quite finish.

Just as I was singing "I'm a reptile, juvenile," there came from in front of the garage a flash and a *ka-boom* and a ball of flame. Somebody screamed. The music stopped. People started running a dozen different ways, and my father grabbed a fire extinguisher off the wall and ran outside.

Whoosh!

In seconds, it was out.

And in a couple more seconds, I heard my mother's voice: "Danny! What's the matter with you, boy? What did you want to go and pour gasoline over your bicycle for? And set *fire* to it! You could've set the garage on fire! You could have burned us all to death! And look! *Look at that!* You're right next to the MG! What if you set fire to the MG? You want my husband to have a heart attack?"

Danny didn't say a word. He looked stunned. I smelled burnt hair. Danny was missing his forelock.

I noticed that my mother hadn't said anything about the possibility that Danny could have hurt himself, too, as if she wasn't at all concerned about that. And she probably wasn't. She was too angry.

Geraldine came out of the crowd. She gave Danny a painful look, as if she had a cramp in her stomach. Without speaking, she reached out and touched his forehead where the hair had burnt off. Danny just stood there, watching her. Then without a word she took his hand, and they walked away, hand in hand, down the driveway.

The crowd was left to stare at a smoking, blackened bicycle surrounded by a puddle of foam.

As I watched Danny and Geraldine walk out of sight, I was thinking that I didn't ever want to fall for a girl. Not if it makes you act like that. And yet I was also thinking: That's what rock and roll is all about. It's not about sex and drugs. It's about whatever it is that makes you set fire to your bike and walk off hand in hand.

KISSING AND STUFF

I lay awake in my sleeping bag. Uncle Earl was in one of the quieter stages of his sleep, simply snoring, sounding like a chain saw that wouldn't start. In my mind I was reviewing everything that had happened that evening from the first note we played to the last wisp of smoke. I felt a song coming like the wailing of a distant siren in the night.

He poured gasoline
On the back tire
And then with a match
He set it on fire.

Do you see the explosion, the bright ball of flame?
Then let me tell you: Love is no game.

Between snores from Uncle Earl, I heard sounds from the kitchen. I got up and found my father, drawing like a madman. As I watched from the doorway, he sketched a rough panel, then another and another. His pencil seemed to be in a rush to keep up with his brain. I walked up behind him, but he didn't notice. Peering over his shoulder, I saw that he was drawing children. One was a tall girl with Afro hair. She looked like Geraldine. Another was a brown-skinned boy with a bicycle. Like Danny. And another was chubby and carried a briefcase. Guess who? There was a white boy with hedgehog hair — like Boone — and a surfer type in sandals and shorts — like Law — and a hip-looking dude with a turtleneck and sunglasses — an exaggeration of Dylan — and a girl with Asian features who wasn't like anybody I knew. Each panel told a little story that wasn't a joke, exactly, but it made you smile because you recognized something true from your life. Or at least, it was true from my life. In fact, it was *stolen* from my life. He was telling stories about me and my friends.

I went back to my sleeping bag without my father ever knowing that I had watched him.

In the morning when I walked into the kitchen, a pile of drawings lay on the table. My father was sprawled sleeping in a chair, mouth open, eyes closed. My mother, in a bathrobe, sat drinking a cup of coffee, reading from the pile and chuckling quietly to herself.

In the afternoon, Boone came over to help clean up the garage. His dog followed him. Boone swept the paper cups and other garbage into a pile while I gathered pop bottles for recycling and the dog licked at a place where somebody had spilled a drink. Suddenly the dog wagged his tail and ran out of the garage. A minute later when we looked up from our work, there was Danny in front of the garage with a Crescent wrench and a can of oil, trying to salvage his bicycle, while the dog lay at his feet. Danny hadn't said a word to either of us. He'd simply come and started working.

"Hey, Danny," Boone said in a friendly way.

Danny didn't look up from his bike. He didn't want to meet our eyes. "Sorry," he mumbled as he squirted oil onto the axle. "I didn't mean to mess up your show." He wiped his shirttail over the seat, then seemed surprised when the shirt turned black. "Dsh," he said.

Boone and I exchanged a look. We hate it when Danny gets down in the dumps. He's had a tough life — all the bad breaks. But he's always bounced back.

"What are you sorry about?" Boone said. "Those were great special effects. Most bands would have to pay thousands of dollars to put on something like that. Now nobody will ever forget our first performance."

"Too bad you ruined the bike," I said.

Danny looked up. "It ain't ruined," he said. "I'll fix it."

My mother walked toward us from the house. She was wearing an apron, and there was flour in her hair. She'd been making pies. As soon as he saw her, Danny's gaze plunged down to the bicycle and stayed there.

"Danny!" my mother said. "Are you all right?"

"Yeah," Danny said. He didn't look up from the bike.

"Did you get burned last night?"

"No."

Now if I were answering those questions, I'd say "Yes, ma'am," and "No, ma'am." I find that if I'm polite and respectful, it softens people. In fact, sometimes it makes them ill at ease, too, which can work to my advantage. It probably would have made my mother apologize for yelling at him last night. But that isn't Danny's style. He's too proud.

"If you're going to work on that bicycle," my mother said, "you'd better move it farther away from the MG."

"All right," Danny said, and he moved the bike about ten feet away.

My mother still looked skeptical. I knew that as long as Danny had a wrench in one hand and a can of oil in the other, she would be nervous. She always worries when Danny comes over. She's afraid he'll break something, or, worse, that he'll try to fix it.

My mother turned to me. "I'm making pies," she said. "No lard, Baba. I've got three pocket pies you boys could take with you if you wanted to go somewhere."

Danny loosened a nut on his bicycle. "We could just eat them here," he said.

He didn't get it.

My mother frowned. "These are traveling pies," she said. "I only give them to boys who are going someplace."

"We could go down to the lake," Boone said. "You could roll your bike, Danny. It's all down-hill."

"The wheel's stuck," Danny said. "Anyway, the tire's burnt."

"I'll help you *carry* it," Boone said.

I think Boone likes my mother's pies even more than I do.

As it turned out, to my surprise, when we sat down by the lake and ate, the pie didn't seem all that good to me, though my mother made it the same way she always does — except without lard. Somehow today it seemed too sugary and buttery. Was I coming down with some disease that was changing my taste buds? How could *anything* have too much sugar and butter?

Danny and Boone had no complaints, though. They licked their fingers, and then Boone skipped rocks on the water. Danny went back to work on his bike, and I asked him, "Where did you go with Geraldine after — you know — after . . . ?"

"We just went for a walk," Danny said. He was trying to get the rear wheel loose from the frame, but the fire had welded them together.

"Where'd you go?"

"Oh. Around."

"*Where?*"

"Little Baldy."

Little Baldy was a grassy hill outside town with some old graves on top.

"What did you do there?"

Danny stopped working and looked at me over his shoulder.

I was being nosy. But I wanted to know for the song I was writing.

"What's it to you?" Danny asked.

"Just wondering," I said.

Danny went back to work on the rear wheel. "She wanted to kiss and stuff," he said.

"What stuff?"

Again Danny looked over his shoulder. "I ain't gonna brag."

"Just tell me."

"Tell you what?"

"*What stuff?*"

"Just . . . stuff. You know."

I didn't know. That is, I'd seen movies, but the boy-girl scenes in movies seemed about as far from the real world as space aliens and superheroes and all the other stuff you see on the screen. The fact is, I'd never kissed a girl. I'd never *wanted* to. It had never even occurred to me that I might *ever* want to or that any of my friends would ever want to.

But Danny had.

And now I knew that someday I would want to. And when I wanted to, I would do it. The thought amazed me. But I knew it was true.

Suddenly a dragonfly buzzed by my nose and landed on a weed. It was a deep, dark, sparkling yellow. Danny squirted more oil on the axle of the rear wheel, and Boone skipped another rock, and I stared at the dragonfly thinking how precious is your flash of life — *dragonfly, dragonfly, short to live and long to die* — and I felt a wave of joy that I couldn't explain except to say I knew that all the songs of all the tomorrows were in my heart today.

WOW

For dinner my mother made beans — without meat. It was my first chance to talk to Uncle Earl since the show, and I asked, "What did you do with the money you collected in the hat?"

Uncle Earl fell back against his chair as if I'd hit him with a brick.

"I'm not accusing you of anything. I was just wondering —"

"I used some of the money to pay myself back for the drinks I bought at the store. The rest is yours, and here it is." He fished in his pants pocket and dropped a handful of coins and a few one-dollar bills on the table.

"Thank you, sir."

"Never give a free show." He stabbed a finger at me to make his point. "Never. Nothing is done for the love of it."

My father raised an eyebrow. "Nothing? Nothing is done for the love of it? Are you an expert on love?"

"That I am, Brother-in-law, that I am. I mean, of course, since you are married to my sister, you know something of love, too. But in the time that you have been in love with just one woman, I have loved dozens. Dozens, Brother-in-law. And that makes me far more of an expert than you."

More L-word. But what they were saying had nothing to do with rock and roll. "Is it true you played drums for Chuck Berry?" I asked.

"Oh yes. Chuck Berry," Uncle Earl said. "Chuck Berry didn't have no band. No traveling band. When he came to a city, he hired local musicians for a concert. The music wasn't as good, but it didn't cost as much. That was his choice. He was a tough man to work for. I played for him once in Louisville. Not very well — but then, not for very much money, either. He got what he paid for. So, yes, I played drums for Chuck Berry. It always seems to impress people, but it ain't the high point of my life."

Something I realized was that my uncle had two different ways of talking. Most of the time he'd speak regular English, and then suddenly he'd switch to street talk. He could turn it on and off.

My father asked, "What *was* the high point of your life?"

Uncle Earl smiled. "It's yet to come, Brother-in-law, it's yet to come. The next love will be the high point of my life. And I got a feeling it's just around the corner."

"You ready to settle down, Earl?"

"With the right woman, I might."

"A woman with a steady job?"

Uncle Earl scowled at my father. He straightened himself in his chair and with great dignity said, "Don't judge a man by his past."

"How else can I judge him?" my father asked.

"By his future," Uncle Earl said.

We all three — my father, my mother, and I — stared at Uncle Earl sitting straight and proud in his chair. I think we were each trying to see the future Earl. I had to admit, I could believe that he wanted to change, that he wanted to be more — well — more like *us*. Dropping the street talk. Marrying a woman, settling down, starting a family. Maybe even holding a steady job.

Right after dinner, Uncle Earl left the house. Since I'd told him about the town bar, he'd quickly gotten into the habit of going there for the evening. He always stayed until closing.

I woke up when Uncle Earl came home at two-thirty in the morning. I heard his car lurch to a stop in the driveway. I heard faint rustling sounds from the kitchen, and I knew that my father was drawing.

The front door squeaked open and then closed with a bang. I heard my father saying something softly to Uncle Earl. Then a crash.

"Earl, you're drunk."

"I may be slightly intoxiculated."

My father was a gentle man. Anyone could tell that. But right now, anyone could hear from the tone of his voice that he meant business. "There are some things," my father said, "that we will not tolerate in this house."

A raspy whisper: "Yassuh."

And I knew that Uncle Earl could hear it, too.

The next morning there was another pile of drawings on the table, and the bags under my father's eyes were even worse than yesterday. He watched as I looked over what he'd drawn.

"Are they funny?" he asked.

"No," I said. "Not ha-ha funny. But they're *good.*"

"I think so, too," my mother said. "They don't try to force me to laugh. They just make me want to smile. And I think, for the long term, that's better."

At school I passed Kirsten with her two giggling friends and asked, "How was the marathon?"

"Not great," she said.

Her two friends giggled. I'd seen them at our show Saturday night.

"Hey," Kirsten said, "I didn't know *you* were in that band."

"Yes," I said.

"Wow," Kirsten said.

Her two friends giggled.

I walked away. I didn't know how to answer that "wow." And I wanted to savor it. That one "wow" was worth a hundred rehearsals in a dusty garage. It was worth a couple dozen bickerings between Law and Dylan over what song to play and how to play it. It was worth a thousand missed notes by Boone and a million yawns by Mr. Womwad, the guitar teacher who lived on the other side of town.

At home after school, I stood in front of the bathroom mirror, singing without making a sound. I wasn't interested in how my voice came across. I was watching the different expressions I could make with my face and ways I could move my hands and my body.

Somebody knocked on the bathroom door.

"I'm in here," I said.

"All right." It was Uncle Earl's voice. "I'll wait."

I held a stick of Ban deodorant for a microphone. Silently I sang into the mike, studying my face to see if I looked sincere.

Again there was a knocking on the door.

"You still in there?" Uncle Earl called.

"Yes, sir."

"Hurry up."

I thought I looked better if I leaned forward while I sang. Raising my eyebrows made me seem more earnest, but it made my eyeglasses slide down my nose. It was better not to smile. Smiling looked slick. Phony. Like a lounge act, not a garage band.

"What are you *doing* in there, boy?"

"Nothing," I said. "Minding my own business."

"Well, can you mind it someplace else? Or I'm gonna have to mind *my* bidness on your mama's *carpet*."

"Just a minute, sir."

I tried to make myself sweat. Singers on television always had sweat pouring down their faces. But sweat wasn't something I could turn on and off like throwing a switch.

"Hey! Beau! Beauregard Bodacious Babcock. Open the door."

"Just a minute, sir."

I looked out over the audience. They were charging the stage. The security guards could just barely hold them. One final bow, and then I'd have to run for the limousine.

The door was rattling. *Blam blam.*

I set down the microphone, released the lock, and walked behind the curtain.

There stood Uncle Earl. He rushed onto the stage and slammed the door.

As I walked away, I heard, muffled, through the door: "That was *vexatious,* boy. Stick around. We can play some catch. I got a mitt you can borrow."

By the time he came out, I had caught the limousine and was gone. I had absquatulated.

I didn't return to the house until suppertime.

My mother looked proud. "Look, Baba. Look what I made you for dinner."

I leaned forward and stared into the platter. White globs. "What is it?"

Uncle Earl and my father both leaned over the platter, too.

"Catfish?" Uncle Earl asked.

"Tapioca pudding?" my father asked.

"Try it," my mother said. "Don't worry, Baba. It's not meat."

So we tried it. I thought it tasted slightly lemony with a hint of bean flavor. Mostly, I thought, it didn't have much flavor at all. My father chewed thoughtfully, then delicately dabbed his lips with a napkin. Uncle Earl put a forkful in his mouth, chewed, puffed out his cheeks and bulged his eyes, then swallowed.

"Tofu," my mother said.

"I like it," I said.

"I suppose I can handle it," my father said. "Every once in a while."

"How do you like it, Earl?" my mother asked.

"I'm your guest, Sister dear," Uncle Earl said. "So of course I like it." He took a long drink of water. "But I have to say, Sister dear, that if you threw this stuff out in the yard, a cat would *bury* it."

Next day Uncle Earl caught me when I came home after school. He was shining his brown leather shoes. "You want to play catch today?"

"No, sir."

"Don't you play baseball?"

"No, sir."

"Why not? Don't you want to play Little League?"

"There's no Little League here. It's too small a town."

"Oh *man*, that's un-American. Don't you play *sports*, man?"

"Soccer, sir."

"What kind of a sport is that?"

"We have a soccer team, sir. In the fall, we play in a league over the hill."

"Over the hill? Where's that?"

"On the other side of the mountain, sir. In the suburbs."

"Where I come from, over-the-hill means something else. It means *dead*. Like *here*. Soccer? That's no sport. I never heard of *no*body taking bets on soccer. What's with this town? If you can find people to play soccer with, why can't you find people to play baseball with? Don't you know this is *spring,* man. In the spring a young man's fancy turns to — Where you going?"

"To the lake, sir."

"Why?"

"To feed ducks, sir."

"What's that in your hand?"

"A briefcase, sir."

"Oh. Of course. Yes indeed. Is this a *suck,* man?"

"What, sir?"

"You trying to fool me? Draw me into your plan? You want me to think you're going down to the *lake* to feed *ducks* with a *briefcase?*"

"Yes, sir."

"Come on. You can tell me." He winked. "You can trust the Reverend Earl. What you got in that briefcase? *Playboy* magazines?"

"No, sir. Popcorn."

I walked to the lake.

While I was throwing popcorn to the ducks, Kirsten ran by. She waved. Right behind her was a tall blonde woman in a bright purple sweatsuit with a purple sweatband. When she saw Kirsten wave at me, she stared. Her head swiveled as she passed me, and she looked back at me over her shoulder. I waved. She snapped her head around so she was looking forward, and she ran on.

I sat down by the lake. The ducks crowded around me, quacking. One took a stab at my shoelace, then muttered that he didn't like it.

The staring woman in the purple sweatsuit had to be Kirsten's mother. She was the woman who liked palm trees. She stared; I waved. In a way, we'd met.

ATTITUDE

For dinner my mother cooked steak and potatoes. She gave me a bowl of cottage cheese to replace the meat. She looked weary.

My father, though, was beaming. He dug into his steak and said, "I showed my new sketches to the agency today, and they *liked* them."

"Hey, that's great!" I said.

My mother smiled weakly.

My father didn't notice. He continued, "They told me to make a portfolio of finished panels, and they'd try to sell them to newspapers."

"Big time!" Uncle Earl shouted.

"Now I really need a place where I can draw," my father said, "and I had an idea. Earl, I was wondering if as long as you're here — and you don't seem to have anything to do — maybe you could work on converting the garage into a studio. I'll pay for the materials and —"

"With what?" my mother said.

"With the money I get from selling my comics," my father said.

"You haven't *sold* them yet," my mother said.

"But I will. I'll stop working at the car shop and draw up a nice portfolio and —"

He stopped talking and stared at my mother, who was quietly crying.

"I'm sorry," she said.

"What is it?" he said.

"I didn't want it to happen like this," she said. "I wanted to tell you . . . a different way. I wanted us to be happy about it." She dabbed at her eyes with a napkin.

"Are you all right?" my father asked.

"I'm fine," my mother said. "I'm pregnant."

For a moment my father looked shocked. Then his face broke into a big smile. "Why, that's *wonderful*," he said.

"You can't quit your job," she said.

"I don't *want* to quit," he said.

"Don't be angry," she said. "Please don't have a heart attack."

"Heart attack? My heart is filled with *joy*. I'll keep the job, and I'll draw at night — just like I've been doing. It'll be like having two jobs. We'll need the extra money."

"And now," Uncle Earl said, "you need another room. For the baby."

"That's right," my father said, and he looked worried. "How can we — ?"

"I got it all figured out," Uncle Earl said. "I'll fix up the garage, and when the baby comes, Beau can move out there. I bet he'd like that. Wouldn't you like that, Beau Bo?"

My own private little house. "Yes, sir," I said.

"And don't worry about paying for the materials," Uncle Earl said. "I'll take care of that."

"How?" my mother asked.

"Don't worry, Sister dear," Uncle Earl said. "I've got some building funds."

"From the Church of MegaChrist? From the ladies of passionate faith? I don't want those funds."

"I can just borrow from the fund. I can raise more. I've got ideas."

My mother scowled at Uncle Earl as if she had a suspicion about those ideas and didn't approve of them, whatever they might be. But then she turned to my father, reached across the table, and took his hand into her own. She smiled.

He smiled back.

I was embarrassed to look at them, the way they were smiling at each other as if nobody else existed in the whole world. I ate my cottage cheese.

For lunch at school my mother had made me a sandwich of avocado and sprouts. I looked up from my sandwich with sprouts dangling from my lips to find Kirsten standing in front of me.

She didn't have her friends with her. She wasn't giggling. She wasn't doing cartwheels or running. She was just standing there with her freckles and her big ears.

"Um. I was wondering," she said.

"What?" I pushed the sprouts into my mouth.

"Could I listen to your band sometime?"

The band. We were going to practice today, after school.

"Uh. Sure," I said. "Sometime."

"Oh," she said. "Good. Well, uh. Thanks."

"You're welcome," I said.

She walked away.

And I sat there thinking: You *blew* it. You stupid idiot. You could've invited her to come *today*. But I had a feeling Kirsten wouldn't mix with the band just right. Kirsten didn't mix with much of anything in my life. Also, we'd be practicing "Dragonfly." She might hear those words I wrote and think they were about her. Which of course they weren't.

As usual, Dylan was the last to arrive at band practice, but the first thing he said was, "Let's make up another song."

"I've already written some lyrics," I said.

"Great," Dylan said. "I've already got a melody."

"Let's hear it," Law said.

Dylan played the melody he'd been working on. Then I read the lyrics to "Love Is No Game."

He poured gasoline
On the back tire
And then with a match
He set it on fire.
Do you see the explosion, the bright ball of flame?
Then let me tell you: Love is no game.

They turned their back
To the band
And walked the streets
Hand in hand.
She had hair like a bomb and eyes like the wind
Never was danger so feminine.

Ain't gonna brag
'Bout what I do
Just wanna try
Some stuff with you.
Come to the graveyard with your lips and your
    hair.
I'll show you my love if you show me you dare.

"This is about Danny, isn't it?" Boone asked.

"What makes you think so?"

"He may not like having a song written about him blowing up his bicycle."

"Maybe I should change it a little."

"Change it a *lot*," Dylan said. "I've got one line for you. I was thinking of it while I was making up the melody: Kiss me, kiss me, don't you dare to diss me."

Dylan played the melody over and over. Law tapped out a beat. I tried to cram my words in, but they just didn't fit. The rhythm of Dylan's melody just didn't match the words I had written.

"He poured gasoline —"

"No no. Gotta match the stress. Listen. It's DA-da DA-da DO-dee wada."

"HE poured GASoline ON the back tire."

"Sounds awful."

"Get the rhythm. It's DID-da DAH-da DOO-dee wada."

"All right. Dida dada doody wada, and then with a match —"

"No no. Doesn't work. It's NA-ba NA NA."

"AND then WITH a MATCH —"

"Gimme a break!"

"All right. Dida dada doody wada, naba na na."

"Nya nya to you, too."

"Dida dada doody wada, naba no no."

"Go go, man."

"Shiba shaba shooby waba, gaba go go."

"Great!"

It was confusing. I felt dizzy. It was changing so fast. I wrote lines, crossed them out, drew circles and arrows, changed my mind, and Dylan and Law and Boone were shouting suggestions and laughing at mistakes and playing the tune over and over and over. . . .

Danny dropped by.

"Whatcha doin'?" he asked.

Nobody answered.

"Did I say something wrong?" Danny asked.

Boone spoke up: "We were making a new song."

"Can I hear it?" Danny asked.

We looked at each other. Suddenly we all felt bad, as if we'd been talking about him behind his back. But the song had changed in the process of composing it, and I said, "Sure. You can be the first to hear it. And if you don't like it, you tell us, and we won't play it anymore."

"Right," Boone said. "You can veto it."

"Why?" Danny asked.

"You'll see," Boone said.

So Dylan played an intro, and then I sang. As I sang, I listened to the words we had come up with, and it was like hearing them for the first time:

Kiss me,
Kiss me,
Don't you dare to diss me.
Dida dada doody wada
Naba no no
Shiba shaba shooby waba

Gaba go go.
The bright ball of flame
Love is no game.
No game,
No game,
Love is no game.

When we were finished, we all watched Danny, waiting for a reaction. Danny had been sitting on my father's workbench. He slid off, and he said, "You guys putting me on?"

Dylan said, "You don't like it?"

Boone said. "We're sorry, Danny. We won't —"

"Hey," Danny said. "I like it. It's *weird.* But I like it."

"You mean," Boone said, "it doesn't bother you?"

"Why should it bother me?"

"I just thought it might," Boone said.

"The only thing that bothers me," Danny said, "is that it doesn't make any sense."

I didn't say anything. I liked the words better before we put music with them. By working with the group, I'd lost control of the song. It wasn't *mine* anymore. And I could never take it back.

UM. WELL. YOU SEE. LIKE. NO.

Uncle Earl skipped going to the tavern for one night. He sat on the edge of the bed, pulling off his socks. I was already in my sleeping bag on the floor, though I wasn't trying to sleep. I was reading a book.

"We start tomorrow," Uncle Earl said, flipping a sock onto the floor.

I looked up from the book. "Start what?"

"Little League." He turned off the light. "Bring your soccer team. And anyone else who wants to play. We'll practice at the school."

I heard him lie down on the bed. My bed. I said, "Uncle Earl?"

"Yes, Bodacious?"

"Who are we going to play against?"

"Over the hill, like you say. I just called up the league over there and joined us up to them."

I lay quietly for a minute, digesting this information. From the kitchen came the faint sounds of my father at work on his drawings. After a minute, I said, "Uncle Earl?"

"Yes, Bo?"

"I don't play baseball."

"Never?"

"Well, sometimes at school. But I don't run."

"What position do you play?"

"Catcher."

"And you don't run?"

"A catcher doesn't have to run."

"What about when you hit? Don't you run when you hit?"

"No, sir."

"Do you ever get on base?"

"No, sir."

"Where do you bat in the lineup? Last?"

"Fourth, sir."

"Fourth? That's cleanup. You don't bat cleanup if you can't drive in runs."

"I drive in runs, sir."

"But you don't run, Beau Bo. You said you don't get on base."

"I don't, sir. I just hit home runs. That way, I can go around the bases as slowly as I want."

"Home runs? That's *good*. So you're a *slugger?*"

"I try. I have to."

"Do you hit home runs very often?"

"No, sir."

"Do you strike out very often?"

"Most of the time, sir."

"All or nothing, huh?"

"Yes, sir."

"What if you hit it, but it doesn't go over the fence? What if you hit it in the gap for a double?"

"Then I'm out, sir."

"They throw you out at second?"

"No, sir. At first."

For a minute, there was silence. Had he fallen asleep? Then:

"Beau. Hey! Beau Bo Babcock."

"Yes, sir?"

"We've got some work to do. On your attitude."

Before I left for school, Uncle Earl got specially out of bed just to tell me to be sure to tell everybody about the baseball team. He was planning to hold our first practice that very afternoon.

I walked to school thinking: Fat chance I'll tell anybody about this baseball team. What if he had a practice and nobody came?

Uh-oh. A poster stapled to a telephone pole. And then another stapled to a fence. And another on a tree. Uncle Earl had known better than to depend on me for recruiting baseball players. The poster not only announced that there would be a practice this afternoon, but also it said:

VISITS BY MAJOR-LEAGUE PLAYERS!
FREE CLINICS ON BATTING AND FIELDING!
FREE AUTOGRAPHS AND BASEBALL CARDS!

He was lying. He couldn't get major-league players. Uncle Earl would stop at nothing. Where did he get the nerve? He might as well have promised each Little League player a try-out with a major-league scout and a million-dollar contract with the Los Angeles Dodgers.

The worst thing was that I was associated with him. Like my mother said, he's family. And when people found out he was lying — and they would when no major-league players showed up this afternoon — it would reflect on me and my family.

Can you divorce your uncle?

At school, Dylan and Boone were excited about baseball.

"You really believe those posters?" I asked.

"You mean," Boone said, looking shocked, "there isn't going to be a practice?"

"There'll be a practice," I said. "But it's my Uncle Earl. He . . . exaggerates sometimes."

"He knows Chuck Berry," Dylan said.

"He doesn't *know* Chuck Berry," I said. "He played drums for him once in Louisville."

"Wow," Dylan said. "Can you *imagine?*" He took a comb out of his pocket and started working on his hair as he said, "So maybe he could get Chuck Berry to play a date with our band."

"Dylan," I began, "he doesn't even —"

"If he knows Chuck Berry," Dylan said, "he probably knows baseball players, too."

I gave up. I was learning a lesson from Uncle Earl: People believe what you tell them — if you tell them what they want to believe. And if you're ready and willing to absquatulate yourself from time to time.

Dylan and Boone started talking about what it would be like to be up on a stage in some big amphitheater with Chuck Berry duckwalking and hopping around. "It would be like being a part of history," Dylan said.

"I'm glad we have a band," Boone said.

"Nothing's more important than the band," Dylan said. "Right, Babcock?"

I didn't answer. I was watching three girls walking toward us on the sidewalk, giggling. The one in the middle had blonde hair. Freckles. Big ears. I stepped toward them, and without saying a word the girls on each side broke into a furious set of giggling and walked away. Suddenly I was alone with Kirsten — alone, but surrounded by friends, hers and mine, watching from a distance.

"Hey," I said.

"Hey," she said.

I nodded my head toward her friends. "Do they always giggle?" I asked.

She frowned with those dark eyebrows as she said, "Do they giggle? What's wrong with giggling, anyway?"

"It's all right," I said. Which surprised me. I mean, I *hate* giggling. That is, I thought I did.

But when Kirsten indicated that she didn't see anything wrong with it, suddenly I wasn't sure what was wrong with it, either.

I set down my briefcase and put my hands in my pockets. I couldn't think of anything else to say.

"Have you lost weight?" Kirsten asked.

"I dunno." I shrugged.

"You look like it."

"I'm not trying."

"But I think you are."

I didn't want to talk about how fat I was. "What about you?" I asked. "Have you gained . . . anything?"

"No." And she blushed.

I was the one who should have blushed. What a dumb thing to say. But at least it changed the subject.

Now I think Kirsten wanted to change the subject, too. "What's in your briefcase?" she asked.

"Oh. Nothing."

"Nothing? Then why do you carry it around?"

"In case I find something I want to put in it."

"Like what?"

"I dunno. A rock, maybe."

"A rock? Why would you put a rock in your briefcase?"

"If it was interesting. Or valuable. Like if I found a gold nugget."

She wrinkled her nose. She did not think it likely that I would find a gold nugget. As a matter of fact, neither did I.

"If you found something," she said, "couldn't you just put it in your pocket?"

I shrugged.

"The fact is," she said, "you like to be different. And carrying a briefcase is different. Right?"

"Is it bad to be different?"

She didn't answer. Instead, she did a handspring. Then she faced me again and said, "Do you really have *nothing* in that briefcase?"

"Well. No."

"May I see it?"

"Um. Well. You see. Like. No."

She frowned.

"It's just a policy," I said. "I never show it to anybody."

She still frowned.

I didn't like to see her frown. I decided to go for it. "Hey," I said. "Would you meet me at

lunch? So we could — like — have lunch together?"

She looked into my eyes. "Um. Well. You see.
Like. No," she said. "It's just a policy. I never
have lunch with boys." She grinned. And then
she turned four consecutive cartwheels, each
one carrying her farther away.

I looked around and saw that her friends
were giggling. And mine were staring.

I ate lunch with Boone, Dylan, and Danny.
Danny was teasing me about my food. Today I
had cottage cheese with pineapple mixed in.
Just that, and a bag of carrot sticks, and a
dessert.

"Where's the pepperoni?" Danny asked.
"Where's the mayonnaise? Where's the potato
chips? Where's the *grease?*"

"I've got a brownie," I said.

"I'll take that," Danny said.

"Okay," I said, and I handed it to him.

Danny looked shocked. "Hey, I was kidding,"
he said. "Don't you want it?"

"No," I said. "I don't like all that . . . heavy
stuff."

"Can't vegetarians eat brownies?"

"Of course they can. It's just . . . I don't seem to like them anymore."

"Yesterday I saw you throw away a piece of cake."

"It was too . . . rich, or something."

"Next time, give it to me."

As we were talking, I was looking across to where Kirsten was eating lunch with her friends. Each time I looked, she was looking at me. And each time our eyes met, we both looked away. I felt a queasiness in my stomach. And no appetite at all.

TAKING LAPS

Uncle Earl was waiting by the backstop after school. He had a duffle bag full of baseballs, catcher's gear, and a pile of raggedy baseball gloves that looked as if they'd been swept out of a barn. Nobody had brought their own gloves because nobody had seen the poster about try-outs until they were already on their way to school, so we all pawed through the pile of mitts and picked one out. Mine felt like burnt toast. It lay flat as if it had been run over by a steamroller. Most of the strings were broken. None of the other mitts were any better.

There were seventeen kids who showed up for the tryout. Two were girls. One of the girls was Geraldine, which didn't surprise me because she was the star player on our soccer team, and I figured she was probably good at baseball, too. She certainly wouldn't be afraid of a hardball. She wasn't afraid of anything.

The other girl was Kirsten. And for some reason, seeing her there, I felt embarrassed. I stood away from her. I didn't even look at her. I was afraid she wouldn't be good enough, and I didn't want to see her make a fool of herself. Or maybe I was afraid I wouldn't be good enough, and I didn't want to make a fool of myself in front of her.

Uncle Earl looked us over. His eyes stopped at Geraldine and Kirsten, who were standing together. He frowned. He said, "Okay, men, first thing I want you to do is take a lap around the field."

So we ran. Geraldine and Kirsten quickly took the lead. Geraldine was the fastest runner on our soccer team and always led us in laps. Kirsten, being a marathon runner, had no trouble matching her stride for stride. The rest of the boys followed, with Dylan lagging behind and myself, half walking, way behind. Uncle Earl was glaring at me as I finally came in.

One boy asked, "Don't you have any better mitts?"

Uncle Earl stared at the boy. "Okay, men," he said. "Let's take another lap."

So we ran — or in my case, half ran — another lap, girls again leading the way. When we returned, Uncle Earl said, "Tomorrow, men, bring your own mitts. Any other questions?"

"Yes," the same boy said. "Where are the major-league baseball players?"

I cringed. I wanted to hide.

Hands on hips, Uncle Earl stared at the boy. "Okay, men," he said. "Let's take another lap."

There were several groans, but we did another lap — again, girls in front. Kirsten didn't even look winded. When we returned, Uncle Earl said, "I told the major leaguers not to show up until the end of practice. Any other questions?"

"Yes," the same boy said. Somebody made a grab for him, but before they could stop him he asked, "Who's coming?"

Uncle Earl smiled. "Another lap," he said.

More groans. Two boys walked away in disgust. But the rest of us took another lap. Then while some of the boys stood bent over with hands on knees, gasping for breath, and Geraldine stood twisting a curl of her giant ball of hair between her fingers, breathing hard, and Kirsten turned five cartwheels, and I finished walking around the field, Uncle Earl said, "I invited Willie Mays. Any more questions?"

Danny grabbed the boy who had been asking questions, and Dylan put his hands over the boy's mouth, and then there were no more inquiries.

Uncle Earl told us to pick a partner, grab a baseball, and play catch. While we warmed up our arms, he walked among us, seeing what we could do.

We looked awful. The problem was the beat-up old gloves we were using. It was like trying to catch with a Ping-Pong paddle. The ball would hit right on the palm of my hand, but then instead of nestling into a pocket, it rolled right out. "That's all right, men," Uncle Earl said. "I know you'll catch better when you bring your own mitts." Then he looked at Kirsten and Geraldine playing catch with each other and having the same problem as the rest of us. But as he watched them drop ball after ball, Uncle Earl shook his head in disgust.

After we'd warmed up, Uncle Earl — now Coach Earl — assigned us to positions around the field: Danny, first base; Boone, shortstop; Dylan, third base. Kirsten and Geraldine, right field. Me he put at catcher.

Uncle Earl pitched batting practice. When Dylan made a weak throw from third, Uncle Earl said, "You throw like a girl." When Geraldine made a throw from right field to home plate on one hop, he didn't say anything.

On my turn at bat, I completely missed nine pitches — and hit one over the fence in center field. "If you'd swing a little softer," Uncle Earl said, "you'd get more hits."

I shrugged.

Everybody got a turn at the plate — except Kirsten and Geraldine.

"Okay, men, that's all for today," Uncle Earl said. "Come back tomorrow — and bring your gloves."

"Where's Willie Mays?" asked the boy who'd asked the other questions.

"Let's take a lap," Uncle Earl said.

"But —"

"Two laps."

"But you said —"

"Three laps."

The boy couldn't open his mouth again. Danny and Dylan had knocked him down, and I was sitting on his chest while Boone held a hand over his mouth.

Three boys walked away without running any laps. From the way Uncle Earl glared at the backs of their heads, we knew that if those boys ever came back, they wouldn't be allowed on the team.

I was still running — well, sort of shuffling along — on my first lap when everybody passed me on their second. I heard Dylan saying to Danny, "I knew there wouldn't be any major-league players."

"Yeah," Danny said. "Me, too."

And as I shuffled on, I realized that I was learning another lesson about the world as seen by Uncle Earl: If you tell people a suck, they'll know in their hearts that it's a suck even as they go along with it. And they won't blame you for it. They'll say they saw it coming.

Uncle Earl should've been a politician.

I was just beginning my second lap when Kirsten finished her third. I wanted to ask if I could walk her home, but I was embarrassed in front of all the players. Besides, I was afraid she'd say no. And I'd be even more embarrassed to make her wait while I finished two more laps. For the first time in my life, I found myself wishing I was more of a runner. I tried telling my legs to go faster — but nothing happened.

As I lumbered along on my second lap, Kirsten picked up her bright blue backpack, threw it over her shoulders, and then ran off the field and across the parking lot with her ponytail bouncing behind her. I followed with my eyes as she zipped bright as a dragonfly down the road and out of sight.

She ran *everywhere*.

Uncle Earl gathered baseballs and dropped them in the duffle bag. I walked my third lap, all alone.

THE DUKE OF EARL

Uncle Earl was loading the duffle bag into the trunk of his Cadillac when I walked up to him after finishing my laps.

"May I have a ride, sir?"

He didn't answer. He was looking away across the parking lot. I followed his eyes and saw one of the teachers standing at her car: Mrs. Rule, whom I'd had for the last two years, though I didn't have her this year. She was the only black teacher at our school. She was strict. She was tough. She was pretty.

She was locked out of her Toyota. She searched in her purse, then shaded the window with her hands and peered inside. She tried to slip her fingernails between the weatherstripping and the top of the window, and then she shook her hand and frowned at it as if she'd just broken a nail. And by that time, Uncle Earl was at her side.

I stayed at the Coupe De Ville and watched.

I couldn't hear the words that Uncle Earl was saying to Mrs. Rule, but it didn't matter because I could see his body language. He was saying *I want to help you; I think you're pretty; I am gracious and witty and urbane.* He made her smile, which was no easy thing to do with Mrs. Rule. And then in a matter of seconds, with the skill of a professional thief — and it flashed through my mind that maybe he *was* one — he had worked her door open. With a bow and a flourish, he handed her the keys.

She smiled, thanked him, and started to step into the car.

Now Uncle Earl went to work. I still couldn't hear what he was saying, but it had made Mrs. Rule stop with one foot in her car. Uncle Earl was gesturing with his hands and dancing with his body, winking his eye and nodding his head while a stream of words poured out of his mouth. Mrs. Rule sat in the Toyota with the door open and smiled again. I knew what I was watching — charm, in the large, economy size — and I wished I had it for myself. I knew without hearing his words that he was using good English, not street talk. I also knew that Uncle Earl was wasting his time. Mrs. Rule was, of course, a Mrs. She closed the door and listened with the window rolled down, enjoying Uncle Earl's charm, speaking to him in a more relaxed manner than I'd ever seen in her classroom.

At last Uncle Earl patted the side of her car, and Mrs. Rule laughed and rolled up her window, and Uncle Earl walked back to the Cadillac. He looked happy.

"Got a date," he said as he started the engine.

"You? With her? But she's *married*."

"Widowed. Drunk driver wiped out her husband a year and a half ago. The poor woman is lonely and sad. And I can be a comfort to her."

After five minutes, during which *he* had done most of the talking, Uncle Earl knew more about Mrs. Rule than I'd learned from two years of sitting in her class. In fact, as I reflected on it, I realized that her husband had died while I was a student in her class, and she'd never showed it. Not a clue. I don't think she'd missed a single day of school. Maybe it happened over summer vacation. But still . . . I guess she controlled herself and her emotions just as she controlled a class. Fiercely. Absolutely.

But Uncle Earl had made her laugh. Uncle Earl had charm — a trait that did not seem to run in my family. At least, it didn't run to me.

"How do you *do* that?" I asked.

"Do what?"

"*Charm* people. Get them to *talk.*"

Uncle Earl reached for the radio and started fiddling with the knob, searching for a station. He said, "I just have to get in touch with that special part of me. Get in touch with who I am."

"Who *are* you?"

"I'm the Duke. The Duke, Duke, Duke of Earl." He let go of the radio tuner with a satisfied smile. He'd found an oldies station — and guess what song was playing! This man not only had charm. He had supernatural powers.

For the rest of the ride home, he didn't say another word. He drove with a bemused half smile, one hand on the steering wheel and the other stroking his mustache. And, for a change, he drove slowly, though I still made sure my seat belt was buckled.

When we arrived at my house, I noticed right away that something was different. The garage door was open. My father's workbench and toolboxes were outside, covered by a blue plastic tarp. Inside the garage were piles of pink fiberglass insulation and a stack of drywall sheets. The band equipment and Law's drum set were still in the back corner. In front were a cot and some blankets. And then I noticed that all of Uncle Earl's boxes and raggedy old suitcases were out there, too.

"You're going to sleep here?" I asked.

"Got to," he said. "I need the privacy. For my bidness. And you need the room. Until the baby comes."

Who would have the garage when the baby came: Uncle Earl, or me, or my father's drawing? I hoped it would soon become my father's studio, but the news, I learned at dinner, was not good.

We had steak, potatoes, and salad, but all I wanted was salad.

My father seemed tired and gloomy. He didn't even finish his plate.

"Thomas," my mother said, "take tonight off from your drawing. You need a rest."

"Maybe I need a permanent rest."

"Don't say that, Thomas. You're just tired."

"I took my portfolio to the agency today, like they asked me." My father pushed his chair back from the table, picked up his pipe, stared into the bowl, but didn't light it. "They turned me down. They were nice about it, but they turned me down. They said a couple things. First of all, they said they almost never take a cartoon strip unless it's already established itself with a local paper. So they were just stringing me along all this time. They could've told me that before."

"So do it," I said. *"Establish* yourself with a local paper."

"It's not that easy." My father was still staring into his unlit pipe. "They said I couldn't have a character who was black, another who was Latino, another white, another Asian, and not have racial conflict. They said it wasn't realistic."

"They be right," Uncle Earl said. "It ain't real."

"Earl," my father said, looking him in the eye, "it's all in your point of view. My cup is half full. Yours is half empty."

"Either way," Uncle Earl frowned, "it's only half a cup."

For once I found myself agreeing with my uncle.

My father shrugged as if to say, Have it your way. On a normal night, he'd argue for his point of view. Tonight, he just shrugged. He looked beaten. His drawing cup wasn't even half full. It was drained.

That night I slept alone in my room, in my very own bed, with nobody's thrashing and snorting to keep me awake, but I woke up anyway. I got out of bed and looked out my door. There was no light on in the kitchen.

I felt that a light had gone out in my father, as well. Lying in bed, I felt a darkness creeping into my entire family. And in that darkness I heard a sad tune that, after a while, turned into a song:

Alone in the bedroom, four hours 'til dawn
Rainy day coming, sunny days gone.
Shut up, birds, don't sing me no coos
Light's off in the kitchen, Papa's got blues.

TAKING SIDES

As I passed the pond on my way to school, I saw a nest where for the last two days a mallard duck had been sitting. This morning, it was unguarded. I walked toward it. I wanted to sneak a peek and find out how many eggs she was incubating.

I found seven. All broken. Not hatched, but broken. Raided. Eaten. Some raccoon, or fox, or snake, or somebody's dog, *something* had murdered seven unborn ducklings.

I thought of my mother going off to work this morning in her van, patting her belly and saying, "Time for us two to be moving."

I wanted her to come home right now, come home and be safe. I wanted her to stop driving a van where there were crazy drunks on the highway.

And I knew she wouldn't. We needed the money. And besides, she wasn't the kind of person to sit around home doing nothing.

To look at the ducks, you couldn't tell that anything had happened. They went about their business on the water just as Mrs. Rule had gone on teaching her class after her husband had died.

Maybe it didn't bother them, but it bothered me. I was depressed.

Snake in the night, warm eggs he can steal,
Headlights come at you, drunk at the wheel,
Babies ain't cheap, the lawyer will sue,
Light's off in the kitchen, Papa's got blues.

I sat down on the steps in front of the school, opened my briefcase, and wrote down the words from my head.

"So *that's* what's in the briefcase."

It was Kirsten, standing behind me and above me on the next step. She was holding two books and a baseball glove.

I slammed the briefcase shut.

"Papers," she said. "Just *papers*. Somehow I thought it might be more exotic. Like, shrunken heads or something. What were you writing?"

"Nothing," I said.

"It looked like poetry." Her eyes were wide. "Do you write *poetry*?"

"No."

"Oh." She seemed disappointed.

"You *like* poetry?"

"Don't you?"

"I — uh — I don't know." I felt flustered. Kirsten had a way of doing that to me. It's a feeling I don't like. But I'd never met anyone before who admitted to liking poetry. And I'd never even considered the idea of whether I liked it — much less that I was *writing* it. "I was writing a song," I said. "I guess it looks like a poem."

"May I see it?"

I flinched. But I said to myself, She likes poetry. She won't make fun of you. Go ahead, stupid.

I opened the briefcase. She sat down beside me on the steps, and I handed her "Papa's Blues." The ink was still wet on the last verse.

She furrowed her eyebrows as she read it. I cringed. She may like poetry, I thought, but she won't like *this*.

When she looked up from the paper, she smiled. "Show me another."

"Do you like it?"

"I'd like to see more."

"Later."

"At lunch?"

"Sure."

She bounced away, and I was wondering: What am I writing blues for? It's a wonderful day.

At lunch we sat alone together. In the distance, Kirsten's friends giggled. Mine stared. I didn't care. *Sproing. Sproing.* I opened the latches of the briefcase and handed her some songs. I didn't show her "Dragonfly." I didn't want to give her the mistaken impression that I was thinking about *her* when I wrote about freckles and big ears.

As she read, she chewed on the end of a lock of hair. When she finished, she looked up, spat out the hair, and handed the papers back to me. "Thank you for letting me see your poems."

"Songs."

"Whatever," she said.

Did she *like* them? I was afraid to ask. Maybe I'd just made a complete fool of myself in her eyes.

I looked around. Kirsten's friends were watching us, and as soon as they saw me looking at them, they giggled.

"Do your friends always giggle?" I asked.

Kirsten looked at them. Immediately they turned their eyes away — and giggled.

"I guess they do." She furrowed her eyebrows. "They're immature."

Before, I'd asked her the same question, and she'd acted as if there was nothing wrong with giggling. I had the feeling that she'd just chosen sides. My side.

Kirsten looked over at my friends. They were staring. When they saw us looking, they turned away.

"Do they always stare?" Kirsten asked.

"No," I said.

She frowned.

"They're a good bunch of guys," I said.

She didn't look pleased. I had the feeling that in her opinion I'd just chosen sides, too. *Their* side.

I wanted to be on her side, too. I wanted to be on *both* sides. Did I have to choose?

"After baseball practice today," I said, "if you're in a hurry like yesterday, you don't have to run off. I could get you a ride with my Uncle Earl. He could drop you off at your house."

"I want to run," she said. "What's the point of getting a ride? As soon as I get home, I change my clothes and then go out and run some more."

"Where do you go?"

"We usually run the forest trail up to the reservoir and back."

"We? Your mother?"

"Yes."

"I saw you the other day. She *stared* at me. Does she run in marathons, too?"

"No. But she won't let me run in the woods alone. She's my chaperone. It's getting hard for her, though. I keep getting faster. She's —"

"Getting slower?"

"No. But she isn't getting any faster, either."

Then I said it. I just opened my mouth, and out it popped. "I'll be your chaperone."

Kirsten looked me up and down. "I don't think it would work," she said.

What was I saying? Was I volunteering to *run?* Me? Of course it wouldn't work. It would be a *disaster.* I couldn't believe the words that were coming out of my mouth, and yet I was saying, "I could practice. I could get faster. Or I could ride a bicycle. Then I could —"

"It still wouldn't work," Kirsten said. "My mother wouldn't — um — wouldn't want — sort of — you know . . ."

I knew. In other words, Kirsten was trying to say that I was exactly what her mother was chaperoning *against.*

I was beginning to wish I hadn't met Kirsten for lunch. I'd made a fool out of myself.

Then Kirsten touched my hand. "I like your poems," she said softly.

And suddenly I didn't care whether I made a fool of myself or not.

"There's just one problem," Kirsten said. "If we're going to be friends, I can't call you Babcock."

"Why not?"

"Because it's *stupid.*"

"That's my *name.* Don't call it stupid."

"But it *is.*"

I stared at her. I was thinking that nobody

else could get away with calling my name stupid.

Kirsten cocked her head and stared back at me. She said, "Don't you have some other name?"

"Danny calls me Badger."

"What do your parents call you?"

"Baba."

"Is that from the song? Ba-ba-ba, Ba-barbara Ann?"

"No."

"Do you have any other name?"

"Well. My uncle. But. Never mind."

Kirsten got a twinkle in her eye. "It must be good, if you don't like it."

"You like Beauregard? Beauregard Bodacious?"

She frowned. "You're right. That's terrible."

"He calls me Beau Bo, for short."

The twinkle came back. "Close," she said. "Your uncle was close. And now I know what to call you."

"What?"

"It sounds like one of your songs. It's time to go, Baba Beau Bo. I'll see you at baseball practice."

When she left, I realized I hadn't taken a bite of lunch. And didn't want to, either.

All during history, I stared at a blank sheet of paper. I didn't hear a word that the teacher said. In my mind I was singing the same words, over and over. At the end of the lesson, I wrote them down:

It's time to go, Baba Beau Bo.
I'll see you at baseball practice.
It's time to run, so move your bun.
Give me a little slack, Miss.

NO DRINKING, NO SMOKING, NO WOMEN

Only ten people showed up for the second baseball practice. The boy who had asked so many questions — and caused us to run so many laps — did not return. Uncle Earl opened the practice by telling us that tomorrow would be our first game. "That means you're in training," he said. "You know what that means? It means no drinking, no smoking, and no women on the night before a game. You understand?"

Boone raised his hand. "You mean, I can't have a glass of water?"

"No alcohol," Uncle Earl said, looking exasperated. "And no cigarettes."

We all looked at each other. None of us drank or smoked, anyway. Come on, Coach. We're only thirteen.

"And no partying all night with those pretty little women," Uncle Earl said.

Danny raised his hand. "What about pretty little girls?" he asked with a grin.

"Take a lap," Uncle Earl said.

We ran.

Uncle Earl had a cardboard box at his feet when we came back from the lap. "You each get a shirt and a hat," he said.

"What's our name?" Boone asked.

"We have a sponsor," Uncle Earl said.

"Who?" Danny asked.

"Couldn't get the grocery," Uncle Earl said. "Couldn't get the restaurant. Bar said they'd do it, but Little League won't let no bar sponsor a team. I'll tell you, men, we almost didn't have a sponsor."

Then Uncle Earl passed out the shirts and hats. And on each one was the name: WORM FARM.

Uncle Earl told us to warm up by throwing the ball around. While we played catch, he walked among us, sneering, saying we threw like a bunch of girls. Kirsten and Geraldine were throwing to each other. Uncle Earl ignored them. At least, today, we were catching the ball.

From watching us throw — that is, watching everyone except Kirsten and Geraldine — Uncle Earl decided that Dylan and Danny would make the best pitchers. He told them to take turns throwing batting practice, with me catching and the girls in the outfield.

After all the boys had batted, Uncle Earl said, "Okay, we done."

That's when Geraldine picked up a bat and walked to the plate. Instead of the usual giant ball of hair around her head, she was wearing a batting helmet, which made her look like a different person.

"I said, 'We done,'" Uncle Earl snarled.

Geraldine faced Dylan, who was pitching. "Throw me one," Geraldine said.

Dylan would do anything to try to please Geraldine. He wound up.

"Throw it *underhand*," Uncle Earl shouted.

So Dylan threw underhand.

Whack!

A line drive to left field.

Uncle Earl stomped to the mound. "Gimme that ball," he said. "I'll show you how to pitch."

Geraldine crouched into her batting stance. Uncle Earl wound up — and fired a fastball as hard as he could throw.

Geraldine swung — and missed. *Pop!* the ball smashed into my glove.

"Ow!" I said.

"Swings like a girl," Uncle Earl said, shaking his head. "Gimme that ball."

I threw back to Uncle Earl. Geraldine crouched. Uncle Earl wound up, just like before, but this time he snapped off a curveball that started right toward the center of the plate, then broke outside.

Geraldine swung and missed. I lunged for the ball but missed it, too. I wasn't used to curveballs. None of my friends could throw one.

Geraldine set her jaw. She crouched. Uncle Earl wound up. This time he fired a fastball up and in, right at her chin. Geraldine spun out of the way. Then she dug back in at the plate, glaring at Uncle Earl. Uncle Earl glared back. He wound up, gave the same big pitching motion, but let go with a change-up. The ball was floating right toward the center of the plate. Geraldine swung. She was way out in front of the ball and missed it completely.

"Strike three!" Uncle Earl said. "You're out."

He looked at Kirsten. "You want a turn, little girl?"

Kirsten shook her head.

"That's not fair," Boone shouted from shortstop.

"Everybody take a lap," Uncle Earl said.

"Nobody in our league can pitch like that," Danny said from first base.

"Two laps," Uncle Earl said.

"You should give her a chance," Dylan said. "She's a good player."

"Three laps," Uncle Earl said.

My turn. I was wearing my undertaker smile. I took a step toward Uncle Earl.

Geraldine stepped in front of me. "Everybody shut up," she said. She took off the batting helmet. I could see that her hand was shaking. But she didn't say anything to Uncle Earl, and she didn't want us to say anything, either. She ran the three laps, beating everybody around the field, even Kirsten. I, of course, came last. Still on my laps, I watched Kirsten pick up her books and her glove and run off down the road. Would she come to the first game tomorrow? Did she hate me because my uncle was a pig? Would she tell her mother? Would she ever talk to me again?

133

Uncle Earl gave me a ride home. I sat beside him in the front seat with my arms crossed, fuming. Finally I said something that wasn't exactly diplomatic. "You know," I said, "you're really an asshole, sir."

Uncle Earl looked at me for several seconds. I was afraid the car would run off the road. Then he looked back out the windshield.

I said, "What's your problem with girls?"

"Girls can't play baseball, Beau Bo. They don't have the muscles for it. The arm muscle." He stroked his mustache, and then he said, "You're sweet on that little blonde girl, aren't you?"

How did he know? I hadn't even spoken to her at either practice.

Uncle Earl was shaking his head. "I see trouble coming," he said with a sigh. "Big trouble for Beau Bo Babcock."

"What trouble?"

"She ain't good for you."

"How do you know?"

"Trust the Reverend Earl."

"What's wrong with her?"

"She's different."

I couldn't believe it. "Different? *You* are calling *her* different?"

"Exactly," he said. He was looking at me, not

watching the road. "You don't even know who she is. And who you are."

"She's an American girl. And I'm an American boy."

"You're an *African*-American boy. But I'm not talking race, here. I'm talking . . . different." Uncle Earl glanced at the road ahead, then looked back at me. "Don't you know she's blonde?"

"So?"

"Listen, Beau Bo. White is a different *race*. Blonde is a different *species*."

"Look out!"

Uncle Earl glanced back at the road just in time to swerve around a corner. Then he stared back at me and said, "You know what makes an animal a different species? You may see two sparrows, or two butterflies, or two *sow bugs* that look exactly alike to your eyes — same size, same color — but they won't mate with each other. Because they see a difference. And in science, if they won't mate, they're a different species."

"I'm not talking about *mating*."

"But you like her?"

"Yes. Please look where you're going. Yes, I like her."

Uncle Earl looked out the windshield. "I want *you* to look where *you're* going, Beau Bo. If you like her, we *are* talking about mating."

"I'm not even *thinking* about —"

"I'm just explaining science, boy."

I folded my arms and looked out the window. Uncle Earl knew as much about science as I knew about Charm. His science was wrong, too. Different species can mate — they can even bear offspring — but they can't bear fertile offspring. Like when you mate a horse with a donkey — different species — you get a mule. But what was the point of arguing with this — this jackass?

When he parked the car in my driveway, he said, "I got something for you."

More advice? No. He pulled a wristwatch off his arm and held it out to me. "Take it, Beau. I want you to have it."

It was the old kind of wristwatch: hands that moved with a soft ticking sound.

"Why, sir?"

"For peace. For friendship. For family. For to give you a touch of *class*."

"Thank you, sir." I slipped it on my wrist. It shone. It did give me a touch of class.

"Take good care of it. It's worth a few hundred."

"*This?*"

"Only the best."

"You bought it?"

"Fixed it."

"Is it *stolen?*"

He gave me a sour look. "I told you. I *fixed* it."

"I won't wear it if it's stolen."

"*Damn,* boy. I swear. It ain't."

A phone was ringing. Uncle Earl raced to the garage and picked up the receiver of a brand-new red telephone.

Jotting something down in a pocket notebook, he hung up the phone and hustled back to the car. "Gotta go," he said. "Tell your mama I won't be here for dinner. I got bidness."

"Where are you going?"

"To the tavern."

"That's business?"

"It's a thing," Uncle Earl said, stepping into the Cadillac with the crumpled fender.

On my wrist, the watch felt solid and snug.

I woke up in the middle of the night. My body was trained to expect Uncle Earl to come in and switch on the light at two-thirty in the morning, and it woke up automatically.

Lying in bed, I heard a car pull into the driveway, a door slam, and Uncle Earl's footsteps walking to the garage. And then his phone rang. Who would call him at two-thirty in the morning? It must have to do with his bidness thing.

Then the house was silent. Almost. A chair scraped in the kitchen.

Ah. *Good.* My father. *He was drawing again.* Even if he was wasting his time, if he'd never sell a cartoon strip in his life, it made me happy to hear that sound. I wanted my father always to have a dream. Because without it — and last night I'd seen him without it — he was a sad, tired, broken man.

THE BUNT SIGN

My father joined me in Uncle Earl's car for a ride over the hill to the game. Normally, my father prefers to drive his MG, but it only seats two.

When we arrived at the playing field, my father went to the bleachers while I joined the other kids on the team. We were all looking around at the nice green grass, the white chalk lines, the real dugouts, the honest-to-goodness pitcher's mound — and we were scared. It was so different from our practice field with the weeds, the gopher holes, the cardboard bases, and the unmarked foul lines we were always arguing about, we felt as if we'd just walked into the big leagues. And there were bleachers with *people* in them. People *watching* us play in uniforms that said WORM FARM.

A silver Buick station wagon pulled into the parking lot, and out stepped Kirsten and a tall blonde woman. Kirsten ran to the field while her mother walked to the bleachers and sat down right next to my father. He must have seemed safe compared to some of the scruffy-looking people up there. Besides the parents of kids on the team, I recognized a group of men who weren't parents of anybody and who weren't exactly the most upstanding citizens of San Puerco. They were the bar crowd. Why had they driven all the way over the hill on a Saturday morning, unshaven, sitting in the sun with six-packs and potato chips, to watch a Little League game?

Uncle Earl called the Worms together for a meeting. He announced our positions and the starting lineup. With ten players, there was only one starting on the bench: Geraldine. Kirsten was starting in right field and batting ninth. Danny, pitcher; me, catcher; Boone, shortstop; Dylan, first base.

"Now we need some signs," Uncle Earl announced. "When you guys are batting, I'll be coaching third base. Look down to me before every pitch. I'll keep it simple. Just two signs. If I touch my hat, it's the steal sign. If I touch my chest, it's the take sign."

Boone asked, "What about a bunt sign?"

"Don't need no bunt sign," Uncle Earl said. "Don't want no bunts."

"But what if we need to advance a runner?" Boone asked. "What if you want a squeeze play?"

"Don't want no sacrifice. Don't want no squeeze play. I want you to *hit* the ball."

"But *every* team should have a bunt sign."

"All right," Uncle Earl said. "What do you want for a bunt sign? Name something. But I ain't gonna use it."

Suddenly Geraldine spoke up. "Picking your nose," she said.

Uncle Earl stared hard at Geraldine. "All right," he said. "If I want you to bunt, I'll pick my nose."

"Good sign!" Boone said.

"Don't want no bunts," Uncle Earl muttered. We were the visiting team, so we were up first. Their pitcher seemed nervous. He walked the first three batters: Boone, Danny, and Dylan. Then I came up. The first three pitches were balls. I looked down to Uncle Earl, expecting him to touch his chest for the take sign, but he didn't.

The pitch came right down the middle of the plate. I swung with all my might. And missed.

Again I looked down at Uncle Earl. No take sign. The pitch came high but in the strike zone. I swung as hard as I could. And missed.

Now I had a full count. I didn't even check Uncle Earl for a sign. The pitch came inside, too close to take but not good to hit. I swung hard — and hit a foul popup on the first base side. I stood at the plate. There was no point in running. The first baseman settled under it and caught it. The crowd cheered. The first baseman looked startled at the cheering and glanced at the stands. Suddenly Boone slid between my legs and touched home plate. He'd tagged up! The catcher shouted. The first baseman whirled and threw home. The throw was wild. Danny and Dylan scored — Dylan, all the way from first base.

Danny slapped my hand. "You got three RBI's on a foul popup," he said.

Uncle Earl called to me from the third-base coach's box: "You're pulling your head. Ease up, and keep your eye on the ball."

When we took the field in the first inning, we gave up six runs. Danny walked four batters. Boone made two errors; Dylan one. I allowed seven stolen bases without throwing out a single runner, and I had a dozen passed balls. Uncle Earl was shouting, "You play like a bunch of old women!" One player struck out, one was called out for passing another baserunner, and one flied to right field — where Kirsten caught it.

The people in the stands were happy. Big cheers had greeted every run. It seemed to me that the lowlife bar crowd had been cheering the runs, too. Didn't they understand the game? Didn't they know that we were their team? Why would they drive all the way over here to cheer *against* us?

In our at bats, Kirsten walked. Uncle Earl made sure she would walk by giving her four consecutive take signs. At first base I saw her checking Uncle Earl for a steal sign, but I knew he wouldn't give it to her. She scored anyway, on a double by Boone. Danny struck out. Dylan walked. Then I came up with runners on first and second. This time I took Uncle Earl's advice and eased up on my swing a bit. *Ting!* The ball popped off the aluminum bat over the first baseman's head and rolled into the right-field corner. And I ran. I really tried. I told my legs to move as fast as they could, and I bent my head and pumped my arms — and I barely made it to first base ahead of the throw. Meanwhile, both runners had scored.

I stood on the bag, gasping for breath, looked over at Uncle Earl — and saw him touch his hat. He was looking right at me and deliberately touching his hat. He wanted me to steal. He'd seen how I ran to first base, how I just barely made it while Dylan who was no speedster ran three bases, and now he wanted to humiliate me. In front of my father. In front of the team. In front of Kirsten.

The pitcher wound up, let go — and I stayed on the bag.

Uncle Earl glared at me. With one hand he touched his cap, patting it with big broad obvious motions, and with the other hand he *pointed* at what he was doing.

Now everybody in the ballpark knew what was coming. "Watch the steal," the second baseman shouted.

I had to go. I took off. The catcher missed the pitch. He tossed off his mask. He picked up the ball and fired to second — and threw the ball into center field. The center fielder picked up the ball, looked confused, and held it. "Throw it," the second baseman shouted. So he threw it — toward third. The third baseman caught the ball on two hops and threw to second. I fell into a slide — and just beat the throw.

Uncle Earl clapped his hands. "That's the longest stolen base in the history of baseball," he shouted. "You should be called for Delay-of-Game." And then, looking right at me, he touched his hat again.

So on the next pitch, I took off toward third. "He's going," the second baseman shouted. The catcher caught the pitch and threw to third. The third baseman caught the ball. I was nowhere near the bag, so I stopped. The third baseman ran toward me, so I started going back to second. He threw to the shortstop, so I stopped, then started going toward third. The shortstop threw back to the third baseman, who had to jump up for the ball just as I was coming at him. I tried to dodge, but my shoulder caught his arm, and he spun around and fell with a whump on his back. The ball trickled out of his glove. I walked the rest of the way to third. The third baseman lay without moving on the ground.

The other team's coach gave the third baseman smelling salts and ice and at the same time was yelling at the umpire to call me out for interference, but the ump said it was unintentional and wouldn't call it.

When play finally resumed, Uncle Earl tapped me on the shoulder, and when I looked at him, he touched the bill of his cap.

He wanted me to steal home!

The man was trying to *kill* me. And once again everybody knew he'd given me the steal sign, even the catcher.

I started running for home. I was *tired*. The catcher caught the pitch. He stood up, stepped in front of the plate, and waited.

Naturally, I stopped running. I turned around and headed back to third. The catcher threw the ball. The third baseman saw the ball coming — and saw *me* coming — and jumped out of the way. The ball rolled into foul territory in left field and came to rest under a fence.

"Advance one base," the umpire said. "Ground rules."

So I walked home.

I'd stolen three bases. And we were leading, seven to six. My father was cheering. So was Kirsten's mother. But the lowlifes looked unhappy. I saw two of them pop open new cans.

The next inning, we weren't so nervous. Danny settled down, didn't walk anybody, and we retired the side without giving up any runs.

We played three more innings without scoring a run, though we gave up two. So we came up in the top of the sixth, losing eight to seven. In this league, six innings is a game. It was our last chance. Geraldine was now playing right field, and Kirsten was on the bench. With one out, Geraldine came up and hit a grounder between first and second for a base hit. Danny walked. Dylan grounded out, but Geraldine and Danny advanced to second and third.

Now I was up. If I made an out, the game was over. If I got a hit, two runs would score, and we would be ahead. I looked down at Uncle Earl. No sign, of course. He was excited, though, hopping up and down and clapping his hands and shouting to the runners that there were two outs and they should run on anything. His upper lip was twitching. He tasted victory. After my first out, I'd hit the ball solidly in my other at bats, and I knew I could do it again. Their outfield was weak. All I had to do was get it out there.

When the first pitch came toward me, I swung with everything I had. And missed.

I checked for a sign. Of course, there was none. You don't steal a base or take a pitch in a situation like this. "Ease up!" Uncle Earl shouted. "Don't pull your head."

On the second pitch, I eased up. Unfortunately, it was a bad pitch, low and outside. I hit it foul down the first-base line.

"Two strikes!" Uncle Earl shouted. He was so excited, he was jumping up and down. "Protect the plate! Don't pull your head!"

And then he gave a sign.

I stepped back into the batter's box. I dug in with my feet. The pitcher went into his windup. He threw. I squared to bunt — and fouled it off.

"Strike three!" the umpire shouted.

The game was over.

"What are you *doing?*" Uncle Earl came storming down the third-base line. "Are you out of your *mind?* You don't bunt with two strikes! What were you *possibly* trying to —"

"You gave me the bunt sign, sir."

"I *never* give the bunt sign."

"You did, sir."

"*What* bunt sign?"

"You picked your nose, sir."

Boone came to my side. "We *saw* you," he said.

Uncle Earl froze. He seemed to turn a dark shade of green. His lip began to twitch. Then he said, "Eight laps. All of you." And he walked to the stands.

We ran. My muscles ached. I saw Uncle Earl talking to the low-life bar crowd behind the dugout, and I saw him counting out money and handing bills to each member of the crowd. It looked to me as if he had to write out some IOUs, too.

Driving home, Uncle Earl was in a terrible mood. Meanwhile, my father looked happy. "Nice game," he said. "You're quite a hitter, son."

"How — uh — that woman who was sitting next to you — how did she like the game?"

My father turned around and looked at me. "Why do you ask?"

"Just wondering."

My father turned back around, and he looked at Uncle Earl as he said, "She didn't like having her daughter on the bench for half the game.

She didn't like hearing the coach yelling that they were playing like a bunch of old women. Other than that, she seemed to enjoy the game, though I don't think she understands it. Like, when her daughter drew a walk, she asked me why she wasn't allowed to hit the ball."

"So she talked to you?"

"She seems like a nice lady. Do you know her?"

"I know her daughter."

"Um-*hm*," my father said, and he sucked deeply on his pipe and looked at Uncle Earl. Uncle Earl looked at my father, and without a word they seemed to have shared some understanding.

Nobody spoke for a while.

As we were nearing home, Uncle Earl — casually, without taking his eyes off the road — said to my father, "Say, Tom, I was wondering if you could do me a favor."

"No loans, Earl."

"Think of it as an *investment*."

"No."

Uncle Earl scowled. And drove in silence for the rest of the trip.

*   *   *

After dinner, I watched the grooming of the Duke of Earl. I was hoping to discover the source of his Charm.

He began with a long shower, which I didn't see, but I heard a lot of singing. Next, with a towel wrapped around his waist, the Duke shaved. I stood outside the bathroom and watched through the open door — open so as to clear out the steam. Then he trimmed his mustache with little gold scissors and added a few snips inside his nostrils and his ears. With a golden clipper he trimmed his finger and toe-nails, lifting his foot to the sink so he could work on it. He brushed his teeth, gargled with mouthwash, slapped some lotion on his cheeks, swiped some Ban on his armpits. Finally he walked out, still dressed only in a towel, wafting a minty, soapy smell.

He knew I had been watching him.

"My ablutions," he said.

"Your what?"

"Ab-loo-shuns."

He walked out to the garage in his towel and returned, a half hour later, wearing a dark blue suit with a light blue handkerchief folded so that its top triangle poked out of the breast pocket. On his lapel he wore a yellow rose that he'd snipped from our rosebush, and in his hand he carried a half dozen more. His hair was brushed; his shoes were shined; his skin steamed with the odor of mint and soap.

Still, all the ablutions in the world didn't change the fact that he was going out with Mrs. Rule, who for two years had held me and my class pinned in our chairs with The Look, the glare of eye that throttled words before they could leave your throat, that smashed away smirks and straightened slouches and accepted no excuses.

"You know, Uncle Earl, I don't think she's your type."

"How do you know my type?"

"She was my *teacher*. She's *strict*. She doesn't put up with goof-offs."

"You calling me a goof-off?"

"Well, sir —"

"I deserve some respect around here."

"Yes, sir."

"Let me lay some more science on you, Beau Bo."

Sigh. "No thank you, sir."

"Let me talk about magnetism. North and south poles. You know what I mean?" Uncle

Earl made two fists and pulled them together. He winked and said, "Opposites attract."

On his wrist he wore a shiny gold watch.

How long was he planning to stay? The facts that he had already installed a telephone in the garage, that he was building permanent walls, that he had a job (or "thing") all made me wonder if he was planning to be a permanent guest.

I wouldn't mind.

What? What did I say?

I wouldn't mind if he stayed.

I was getting used to him, getting to think of him as family. As, almost, a brother. An older brother.

After he left, I saw my mother looking at the bathroom sink and frowning. The bowl was coated with a scum of shaving cream, hair, and nail clippings.

"Those are Uncle Earl's ablutions," I said.

My mother shook her head. "Those are his pollutions," she said. She started wiping the sink with a sponge.

LUV AND WAR

First thing Sunday morning before anyone else in the house — or garage — was awake, I put on a sweatsuit and stepped outside. I stretched, not because I felt that I needed a stretch but to put off this crazy idea for another few minutes. Did I really want to? Yes. I did. I put one foot ahead, then the other, faster, a little faster — and I was running.

Me. Babcock. Running.

I started downhill toward the lake. San Puerco is on the side of a mountain, so there's very little level ground. You either run uphill or down. For my first run, I preferred down. One

road that I could follow would take me directly
down to the lake, but I knew that once I reached
the lake there would be nowhere to go but up,
so I took a different street that wound slowly
and slightly downhill through the town. I passed
Boone's house, nestled among giant redwood
trees with a Volkswagen bus out front. I passed
Dylan's, which was up a steep driveway and
built on stilts. I passed Danny's little cabin and
then ran along the valley where Disappearing
Creek disappears, passing the driveway that
wound back to Law's gigantic house. Nobody
saw me this early in the morning, which was
exactly my plan. I didn't want teasing. Or sym-
pathy. I wanted to suffer alone. And I *was* suf-
fering. Sweat was fogging my glasses and
making them slide down my nose. My lungs
couldn't suck air fast enough. My heart was
pounding. I was still going downhill.

I reached the lake and ran alongside it. A few
ducks were asleep in the middle of the road.
They like it there. If a car comes, they'll move —
reluctantly — but as soon as the car has passed,
they settle down in the same spot. I ran around
them. The road started to go up. I ran for a few
hundred feet, then turned and went back down.
I just couldn't run uphill. I ran along the lake

again, weaved among the sleeping ducks, and came to the road I had arrived on. After a couple hundred feet of going up that road, I turned again and ran back down. I felt like a marble settling into the bottom of a bowl.

I heard footsteps behind me. Quickly they were catching up. I heard a voice:

"Hey! Baba Beau Bo!"

In a moment, Kirsten had run up beside me. I stopped. She stopped. Coming up fifty yards behind was her mother, looking exhausted. Which was how I felt, only worse. I was gulping air. Standing made me dizzy, so I started walking. Kirsten walked beside me. She was breathing hard, also, but it seemed natural with her, not desperate. In a few seconds, her mother caught up with us and slowed to a walk, too.

"Kirsten," she said, panting for breath, "you were deliberately trying to leave me behind."

"I'm training," Kirsten said, looking straight ahead. "I shouldn't be *accommodating* to slow runners."

"I am *not* a slow runner."

Kirsten didn't even show that she'd heard. She was looking at me. "I didn't know you were a runner."

"Well. Maybe," I said.

"You want to run in a marathon?"

"No."

"Just conditioning, huh?"

"I guess."

"Mom, this is Babcock. Babcock, my mother."

"I'm Greta Kohler. How do you do." It wasn't a question. Just a statement.

"Pleased to meet you, Mrs. Kohler, ma'am."

We were walking up the road that I'd tried to run up before.

"Where do you run?" Kirsten asked.

"Oh." I shrugged. "Around."

"We *always* go to the reservoir," Kirsten pouted, shooting a look at her mother. "We're in a rut. You're right. We should do something else for a change."

Kirsten's mother looked annoyed. I had the feeling that somehow I'd just joined one side of an argument.

Kirsten's breathing had almost returned to normal. Her mother and I were still panting.

We reached the house with the three palm trees.

"It was nice to meet you," Mrs. Kohler said.

"Would you like to come in and have a glass of orange juice?" Kirsten asked.

Mrs. Kohler looked surprised and slightly displeased.

I followed them between palm trees, around the Buick, and through the front door. Their house was bigger than mine. Their kitchen seemed to have acres of counter space — plus a table and also a desk. My father could draw here and not have to wait for the table to be free. But then, why draw in the kitchen? The house must have plenty of extra rooms.

She wasn't rich. And I wasn't poor. But there was a difference.

"Babcock has only one name," Kirsten said to her mother.

"Oh? That's interesting. That's . . . original." Mrs. Kohler poured orange juice into three glasses. "Do you want ice, Babcock?"

"No, thank you, ma'am."

I was waiting for the inevitable question. Kirsten was watching her mother as if she were waiting for it, too. But Mrs. Kohler simply handed me a glass without asking why I had only one name. Kirsten, when she realized that the question wasn't coming, seemed slightly irked.

"Babcock's a musician," Kirsten said. "He's in a group."

"What kind of music?" Mrs. Kohler asked.

"Mostly classics," I said. "And also we —"

"Classical music?" Mrs. Kohler's eyes lit up. For the first time, she seemed genuinely interested in me. "Are you a quartet? Do you play the violin?"

"Guitar," I said. "Fender Telecaster. I'm in a band. We play classic rock, and also some newer ones."

Mrs. Kohler smiled. "How interesting. What is classic rock?"

"Old songs, ma'am."

"And what makes it classic? I mean, are certain songs simply *old* while others are classic?"

"It's a matter of opinion, ma'am."

"How interesting. Is there an official *list* that a song has to get on before you can call it classic?"

"Not that I know of, ma'am."

"But there must be *something* that makes you call one song a classic and the other —"

Kirsten broke in: "Mother, would you *stop* it?"

"Kirsten, that was *rude*," Mrs. Kohler said.

"*You're* being rude," Kirsten said. "You're pretending to be interested in what he —"

"I'm not *pretending*."

"You *always* try to butt in on —"

"I am *not* butting in."

I wanted to take cover under the table. But as suddenly as the spat had started, it stopped. Mrs. Kohler turned to me with a weary sigh. "I need a shower," she said. And she walked out.

Kirsten watched her go. "I'm sorry. She meddles."

"I should leave."

"Don't you want some breakfast?" She opened the refrigerator. "Bacon and eggs?"

"I don't eat bacon."

"Sausage?"

"No. You see I don't —"

"Corned beef hash?"

"I'm a vegetarian."

Her eyes got wide. She held the refrigerator door open. I could feel the cold air flowing out past my ankles.

"Why?" she asked.

"I don't like killing things."

"Not just dragonflies, huh?"

"Sow bugs, too."

"*Nobody* eats sow bugs." She closed the refrigerator.

"I don't want animals to be killed. That's all."

"But you kill plants?"

"For food, yes."

"Wow."

That was the third "wow" I'd gotten from Kirsten. I didn't know what this one meant.

Mrs. Kohler stepped back into the kitchen carrying a folded pink towel. "Is there anything I can get you before I disappear into the shower?"

"You don't need to check on us, Mother."

"I'm just trying to —"

"We're fine. Except there's nothing to eat."

"Nothing? There's bacon. There's sausage. There's —"

"We're vegetarians, Mother."

Total silence. I don't know who was more surprised, Mrs. Kohler or me. Once again, Kirsten had chosen sides.

Mrs. Kohler recovered quickly: "Do vegetarians drink milk?"

Kirsten looked unsure.

"Yes," I said.

"Do they eat eggs?"

"I do," I said.

"So do I," Kirsten said.

"Then we have something to eat," Mrs. Kohler said. "I could make an omelette."

"You're going to take a shower," Kirsten said.

"The shower can wait."

"You're sweaty, Mother. You *stink*. Take a shower."

"*You* take a shower, Kirsten. Right now. A cold one. Cool off that hot head of yours, and when you come back, I'll have breakfast ready."

"*Forget* breakfast!"

"I will forget *nothing* about this morning."

Kirsten glared at her mother. "I'm not hungry," she said.

Mrs. Kohler glared back.

"Uh. I'd better go," I said.

Nobody tried to stop me.

Back home in my own kitchen I found my father, my mother, and Uncle Earl at the table eating my mother's homemade sweet rolls, drinking coffee, and reading the newspaper. My father spends hours studying the Sunday funnies.

I sat down and found to my surprise that I wasn't hungry. All I'd had was some orange juice at Kirsten's.

My father set down the comic pages and said, "Well, Earl, how'd it go last night?"

Uncle Earl looked up from the sports section and beamed with a smile so broad that it almost closed his eyes. "Ell you vee," he said. "*Luv.*"

My father seemed amused. "In which, as I recall, you are an expert."

"Absolutely. I'm going to marry that woman."

My mother looked skeptically over the top of the front page. She asked, "Does the lucky lady know of your wedding plans?"

"Not yet," Uncle Earl said peacefully. "I thought a first date might be a little — uh — *premature* for a proposal of marriage. Anyway, I need for my bidness to pan out before I can marry."

"Business?" my father asked. "What business are you in, now?"

"It's a kind of investment bidness. I don't really want to talk about it yet. Sporting investment. You'll see."

My father tapped his fingers on the comic pages. He still seemed amused. He said, "And when it becomes a steady job, then you plan to marry?"

"That's right. When I can say I've got work. Can't marry a woman until you've got work."

Suddenly my father looked serious. "You know, Earl, if you really love her, and she really loves you, then you've already got work."

"What work?"

"Starting a family. Keeping it strong. It's the best work a man can do."

Uncle Earl stared at my father. "The best work is something that *pays*."

"It pays." My father picked up the comics. "It pays big time."

FLOWERS

Lunchtime at school, Kirsten and I sat together without any prearrangement. Right away she said, "I'm sorry about my mother."

"She's all right," I said.

"She meddles." Kirsten unzipped her backpack and handed me a sheet of paper. A poem. It had been printed on a computer.

"You wrote this?"

"Uh-huh."

I left my home and flew with the wind
Over the river and meadow
To my own spot of soil

Wet with rain
Warm with sunshine.
Now I am free to grow tall in the light
To curl my toes in the mud.
Lifting eyes to the day
I offer my flower
For you to make honey.

I read it three times.

"Do you like it?" she asked.

"It's wonderful."

She smiled.

"I'd like to show it to the band," I said. "I think we could make a song out of it."

She looked surprised. "But it's a poem."

"I think it could be a song."

"I didn't write it for the band. I wrote it . . . for you."

"But it could be a song."

"You mean you don't like it the way it is?"

"I like it. But we need material. Could we try it?"

"It's sort of . . . personal."

"I won't tell them you wrote it. Okay?"

"Well . . . all right."

I could see the misgiving in her eyes. I had

the feeling that once again, she felt that I had chosen sides. The wrong side. But then she'd said it was okay.

When the band arrived for practice after school, we found Uncle Earl nailing drywall onto the studs of the garage. I asked if he would take a break for a couple of hours.

"Sure, I'll take a break," he said. "I'll help you practice."

Even though I was coming to like Uncle Earl — that is, like him with certain reservations — the idea of him helping the band struck my heart with terror. "No," I said. "No, sir. No thank you. We'll just —"

"Hey, that would be great," Dylan said. "You used to play with Chuck Berry, right?"

So Uncle Earl joined the practice.

"I've got something we could turn into a song," I said. I unfolded the paper and read Kirsten's poem out loud.

When I finished, I looked up and saw four blank faces.

"It doesn't rhyme," Boone said.

"It's got no beat," Law said.

"It's a *girls'* song," Dylan said.

"So sing it in falsetto," Uncle Earl said.

"Hey yeah, right!" Dylan said. "We'll pretend we're *girls.*" Dylan sang in a mocking, high voice: "*I'm a flower. See me, the pretty flower. I curl my little toesie-woesies in the mudsy-wudsy.*"

Law started tapping out a beat. Dylan played some notes on the keyboard and sang: "*I'm a pretty flower with love to share, so sniff my armpits and water my hair.*"

My lip was beyond twitching. My face was beyond smiling. I grabbed Dylan by the neck and knocked the keyboard so it went scraping along the concrete floor.

Uncle Earl hauled me off him.

"This practice is *over!*" I shouted.

"We just started," Boone said.

"You go in the house," Uncle Earl said. "I'll help these boys."

In my room I tried to calm down. I fed Frederick and Douglass, and then I took Martin Luther Kingsnake into my hands and let him slither around my shoulders and neck. All the while, I could hear the muffled sound of drums beating and bass guitar plunking. *My* band was practicing in *my* garage with *my* uncle. Without me.

At dinner I asked Uncle Earl how the practice had gone.

"Not bad," he said. "That Dylan is one cool cat."

"He thinks you were practically Chuck Berry's *partner.*"

"Yeah, he was dancing to my beat."

"What did you tell him?"

"Just that he was cool."

At school Dylan was wearing sunglasses — inside the classroom. He sat at his desk snapping his fingers, nodding his head, singing — whispering — songs that I couldn't hear. He was one cool cat. Uncle Earl had told him so. And Uncle Earl had played with Chuck Berry, and Dylan had practiced with Uncle Earl, so Dylan was practically *famous.* Or so he seemed to feel.

At baseball practice Dylan, still in sunglasses, was snapping the fingers of the hand that wasn't in a baseball glove and singing snatches of songs. When batting and fielding was over and it was time to begin running laps, Dylan picked a dandelion, sniffed it theatrically, and sang in falsetto:

I'm a pretty flower, watch me grow
I'm a pretty flower with mud in my toe
I'm a pretty flower waiting to be cut
Sniff my armpits and kiss my butt.

Kirsten's face went red. She shot me one glare of hate — and another at Dylan — and took off like a bullet running her laps. I tried to run faster so I could finish before she ran away home. During my second lap, she passed me on her third.

"Kirsten," I puffed, "they don't know —"

"Shut up."

"— who wrote that poem."

She didn't hear the end of the sentence. She was too far ahead and I was too out of breath to shout.

I did go faster. I finished just a little behind the other slow runners, which was a big improvement — though it nearly killed me. Kirsten was gone.

Uncle Earl gave me a ride home.

"Team's looking better, Beau."

I didn't answer.

"We're gonna win our next game, don't you think?"

I didn't answer.

Uncle Earl stared across the seat at me. "Try flowers," he said.

"Huh?"

"Give the girl flowers. Take my advice. I been there. I don't know what the problem is between you two, but I know this: Flowers do the job. Do it every time."

"Please watch the road, sir."

He glanced ahead, then looked back at me. "I'm offering the benefit of *years* of experience. Trust me. Flowers work."

"It's corny," I said.

"But it works."

PACIFIC GIANT MALCOLM

I couldn't bring myself to try flowers. It was a matter of pride. I did try to call her, but her mother said she wouldn't speak to me. Which made me mad. Shouldn't she give me a chance to explain? *I* didn't write those mocking lyrics. And I didn't tell who had written the poem, so the band didn't think it was *hers*. As a matter of fact, they must have thought it was mine.

So I brought no flowers to school the next day, and Kirsten hung out with her giggly friends, though whenever I looked at her, I caught her looking at me. And every time, she would quickly look away.

My face must have showed something be-
cause when I came home from school, Uncle
Earl said only one thing to me: "Flowers, Beau.
Flowers."

I took a run — seemed a little faster — returned home. Uncle Earl's hammering in the
garage felt like pounding in my brain. Grabbing
my briefcase, I went to the lake and stood by
the edge of the water. A few ducks paddled over
to see if I had brought food, scolded me when
they saw that I hadn't, and drifted away. The
sun had disappeared below the tops of the trees,
but there was still plenty of twilight.

I was mad. Mad at Dylan for making fun of
the poem. Mad at Kirsten for not letting me explain. Mad at myself for showing the poem to
the band. Mad at Uncle Earl for meddling. Mad
at my mother for making me fat. Mad at the sun
for setting when I wanted light.

A dragonfly buzzed past my face, and I was
mad at it for interrupting.

I wanted to write a song. An angry song. A
rap song with a *boom-chucka boom-chucka pow
pow pow* kind of a feeling. Sitting, leaning back
on my hands, staring above the trees at the pink
sky where one lone dragonfly darted and
danced, to my surprise I made up a poem:

On four fragile wings I fly.
I soar over trees
searching only for you.
My eyes see one thousand facets
of your face.
In the dying sun my body flashes
a desperate silvery blue.
It flashes for you.

I opened my briefcase and wrote it down. I had a feeling it wasn't a very good poem, but it was the first I'd ever made up, and I wanted to keep it.

As I was writing the last line, there was a rustle near my feet. What? There. Look at that! On the bark of an old rotten log stood a *monster* salamander — at least twelve inches long — with slimy purple skin covered by blotches of black. A warty belly like a wrinkled prune; toes like tentacles of fungus. Curious bulging eyes. The powerful jaws were chewing slowly, thoughtfully, on the front end of a banana slug that was dangling from its lips like a yellow cigar.

It was *beautiful.*

Carefully I set the briefcase aside. Slowly I rose to my knees — and then I lunged. Caught it! With its slick skin it almost slipped out of my hand, but I wrapped my fingers around its belly so that its legs flailed at the thin air. It dropped the rest of the slug — and snarled. *Snarled.* I swear. I held it up, face to face, and stared. It opened its mouth and *barked* at me. *Ahack! Ahack!*

It was a Pacific giant salamander. I'd read about them. I'd seen a picture in the Audubon Guide. But this was the first I'd ever seen — in the flesh — and it was mine.

"Your name is Malcolm," I said. I opened the briefcase, held Malcolm inside, slipped out my hand, and quickly closed the two sides. I heard him scuttle from side to side across the bottom.

As I was crossing the road, Kirsten came running down the hill. A hundred yards or so behind came her mother.

Instantly, I made a decision. I'd give her the poem. It was almost as corny as giving flowers, but I didn't care.

"Kirsten, I have something for you."

She didn't stop. She ran right by.

I ran after her with the briefcase swinging at my side. Amazingly — although it didn't amaze me until I thought about it later — I caught up with her.

She glared at me. But she stopped.

I spoke in a rush: "Dylan wrote those words. I had nothing to do with it. I tried to *choke* him. This is all a misunderstanding and a mistake and I have something I want to give to you." Meanwhile as I was talking I was springing open the latches to the briefcase before she could turn away, and as I lifted the lid her eyes fell upon not my poem but what was sitting, slightly dazed from the run, on top of the poem. Malcolm.

Her eyes showed a flicker of doubt. Or disgust. But then before I could open my mouth to explain, her face lit up, and she exclaimed: "Wait until my mother sees *this!*"

I didn't have to wait very long.

"What is that disgusting creature?" Mrs. Kohler asked, joining us as we stood at the side of the road.

"A Pacific giant salamander," I said. "Named Malcolm." I was holding him in my hand. I didn't want to lose him, but if it was the price I had to pay to make up with Kirsten, then I was willing.

Kirsten said, "He's *giving* it to me."

Mrs. Kohler frowned. "Oh dear," she said. "And where will you keep it?"

Kirsten almost smirked as she said, "I'll keep it in the kitchen."

"You will *not*. Anyway, I didn't mean what *room*, I mean what sort of a *cage*?"

I answered, "You need a terrarium. A couple inches of water and some rocks it can climb on."

"And what does it eat?" Mrs. Kohler asked.

"Slugs."

Mrs. Kohler looked at her daughter as if she were appraising a used car. After a few moments of thought, she said, "All right, Kirsten."

Kirsten looked surprised.

"You can keep it in your room," Mrs. Kohler continued. "And every day, you can catch some slugs and drop them in the tank."

Now Kirsten looked worried. "Does it eat anything else?" she asked.

"Snails, I think. And insects. And other salamanders. Oh — and snakes, too. Small ones."

Kirsten looked more and more nervous.

"Go ahead," Mrs. Kohler said. "He's giving it to you. *Take* it from him."

Kirsten looked at the salamander, and then she looked at me. I held out my hand.

Malcolm snarled.

Kirsten started to reach for him, then pulled her hand back.

"Go on, Kirsten," her mother said.

Kirsten reached out again. Gently, I tried to transfer Malcolm to her hand, but he started wiggling. Just as Kirsten's fingers were closing around his belly, he barked.

Ahack! Ahack!

Kirsten jumped backwards and opened her fingers. Malcolm pushed off from her hand, so instead of falling straight down to the ground, he sort of flew toward Mrs. Kohler and landed on her knee. Mrs. Kohler screamed and jumped in the air — and came down on Malcolm's right front leg. I dropped to the ground on my knees and scooped Malcolm into my hand, meanwhile bumping against Mrs. Kohler's thigh and causing her to lose her balance. She turned a somersault over my back and fell facefirst into some mud while my wristwatch cracked against a rock.

Malcolm's leg was crushed. He looked at me with shock and bewilderment. I grabbed my briefcase and ran toward home with the salamander in one hand and the briefcase in the other. It wasn't until the next day that I realized I'd run uphill all the way home. At the time, leaving the lake, all I could think about was getting some first aid for Malcolm.

Behind me, I could hear Kirsten shouting, "Mother, I *hate* you!"

I ran into the house, straight to the bathroom, and placed Malcolm in the sink. I ransacked the medicine cabinet for something I could put on a crushed leg. I was so upset, I think I was actually expecting to find some little bottle that was labeled CRUSHED LEG MEDICINE FOR PACIFIC GIANT SALAMANDERS. It took me a minute to realize I had no idea what to do. I lifted Malcolm and walked to the kitchen where my mother, father, and Uncle Earl were eating dinner.

"We started without you," my mother said. "You're late."

"Sorry, ma'am." I sat down and set Malcolm on my plate. He looked confused. Little strings of body parts were oozing out of the leg.

My father chuckled. "I thought you were a vegetarian."

"I'm not going to *eat* him," I said. "I'm trying to *help* him."

Uncle Earl was out of his chair and standing by the door.

"What *is* that?" Uncle Earl said in a tight voice. "Does it *bite?*"

"It won't eat you, sir."

My mother said, "Get it off the table, Baba."

"Won't somebody *help* me? Its leg is *crushed.*"

My mother looked sympathetic. "You'd better take it to that man."

There was a biologist in town by the name of Dr. Vargas. His specialty was slugs, but he'd helped me before when I needed advice about how to take care of Martin Luther Kingsnake. He told me once that he hopes I'll be a biologist one day, too, and maybe I will if rock and roll doesn't pan out. Anyway, I brought him Malcolm.

Dr. Vargas said a splint wouldn't work. He said he'd have to amputate. And he did.

"Now you'll have to keep him," Dr. Vargas said. "I wouldn't have recommended him as a pet, but you can't return him to the wild with only three legs. Do you have another aquarium?"

"Not yet," I said. "I'll have to buy one."

"Here. Take this." And he gave me one. "He needs to stay moist. Or he'll die. He can't wait for you to go shopping."

"Thank you, sir."

"How did he get hurt, anyway?"

"He barked at a girl. And she dropped him. And her mother stepped on him."

Dr. Vargas shook his head. "The poor *dear*," he said, and I knew he wasn't talking about Kirsten or her mother.

The wristwatch had a shattered crystal. I took it off but didn't say anything to Uncle Earl. He'd be mad.

Walking to school, I met up with Boone and Danny.

Danny could read my face: "So what's the problem, Badger?"

I told them I had a wounded salamander.

"Now that's a *problem*," Danny said.

Was he being sarcastic? I couldn't tell. I wanted his help. Danny was my only friend who might know about girls. (Dylan, of course, *thought* he knew about girls.) Danny had actually taken Geraldine off to the graveyard. Kissing and stuff.

So I told him what had happened — everything — from her writing a poem, to me showing it to the band (Boone overhearing, saying, "I didn't know it was hers, Babcock, I'm sorry"), to my writing a poem for her, and her thinking

I was offering Malcolm instead, to Mrs. Kohler stepping on his leg and falling over into the muck. I said I felt used. I said Kirsten was using me — and Malcolm — to get at her mother. "So what would you do, Danny?"

"You already done it, Badger. Face plant. Beautiful."

"That was an *accident*. That was her *mother*. What would you do about Kirsten?"

"Freeze her."

We had reached the school, and there she was. Kirsten approached me with a big smile on her face and said, "You should have *seen* my mother after she fell in the mud."

I turned my back and walked away.

When I saw Kirsten later in the hallway, she looked hurt. And when she looked hurt, somehow she looked even skinnier — like a stick that could be broken. Her freckles stood out more. Her ears seemed bigger. Her eyes seemed bluer — and very sad. She was chewing on her hair.

I felt bad. She'd bounced up to me like a trusting puppy, and I'd kicked her. I wanted to make her feel better. But I was still angry about Malcolm, too, so I stayed away from her at lunch. I ate with Danny and Boone. Danny was saying, "When I'm sixteen I'm gonna buy a big black Harley-Davidson motorcycle and ride it to Mexico and maybe to Antarctica."

Boone said, "You can't ride a motorcycle to Antarctica."

"Yes I can. I'm gonna see some penguins."

I stopped listening. Kirsten ate with her giggly friends — and didn't do any giggling. I knew because I kept checking on her. And every time I looked, she was chewing on her hair.

The next day at school, Kirsten and I stayed apart. At lunch I asked Danny, "Have you and Geraldine ever had a fight?"

"You mean like beating each other up?"

"No. Like being mad at each other."

"Once."

"What happened?"

"I threw her jacket in a Dumpster."

"Why?"

"For fun."

"What was fun about that?"

"Dsh." Danny shrugged. "You had to be there."

"And she was mad?"

"Yeah."

"What did she do?"

"Cry."

I couldn't imagine Geraldine crying. She was tough as granite. You couldn't hurt her enough to bring tears — not physically. But a jacket in a Dumpster . . . This was *strange*.

"So what did you do, Danny?"

"Took it out of the Dumpster."

"That's all?"

"That was enough."

"How come you never sit with Geraldine at lunch?"

Danny shrugged. "I dunno."

"You like her, right?"

"We hang out some. But you know. We just . . . You know."

I didn't know.

After school, we had a baseball practice. Once, I walked over to Kirsten, trying to come up with something to say.

She turned her back to me.

Would she cry if I threw her jacket in a Dumpster?

This was rock and roll. And I didn't know the chords.

Driving me home, Uncle Earl said, "Did you try flowers?"

"No, sir. But I gave her a Pacific giant sala-mander."

"That thing you had on your plate the other night?"

"Yes, sir."

Uncle Earl shook his head. "Did it work?"

"Not the way I expected."

"Flowers, Beau. Try flowers. Where's your wristwatch?"

"I'm — uh — not wearing it."

"Break it?"

"Yes, sir."

He parked in the driveway. "Bring it to the garage."

I fetched it from my room.

Uncle Earl shoved some boxes out of the way and uncovered a scuffed-up black briefcase. Opening it, he removed some fine silver-col-ored tools. He wedged a magnifying eyeglass over one eye. Squinting, he leaned over the watch. The tools in his fingers moved so fast, I could barely follow with my eyes. In about a minute, he handed me the watch — with a brand-new crystal.

He really could fix watches!

"Uh, thank you, sir."

"You take care of this thing, now. You hear?"

"Yes, sir."

He had long, delicate fingers — I'd never noticed before.

He dropped the eyeglass into his hand. He squinted at me — and I felt he could magnify right into my thoughts. "Don't underestimate me, Beau."

"I won't, sir."

THAT'S A FACT, MISS

Early Saturday morning I rode to the baseball game in the plush though tattered front seat of Uncle Earl's Coupe De Ville. None of the bar crowd showed up. As I looked over the people in the stands, I saw one surprise: Mrs. Rule, with her hair in a scarf and wearing black pants — the first time I had ever seen her wear pants or look casual in any way.

Uncle Earl counted heads and saw that exactly nine players had arrived. He told Geraldine and Kirsten that they would play for the full six innings — in the outfield, batting eighth and ninth. He hit practice balls to all the infielders and to the one outfielder who was a boy.

We played a strong game — for Little League, that is. The big moment for me came when I made a play at the plate. The batter for the other team hit a line drive to the right-field corner. The runner on first base took off and never looked back. I guess he figured he could score easily because in our league you usually find the weakest player in right field, and on our team we had a girl playing out there. What he didn't know was, that girl was Geraldine. She ran the ball down, then pegged a throw on two hops to me at home plate. I caught it, stood on the third-base side of home plate, and waited. The runner had turned the corner and was coming at me, head down. I'd thrown off my catcher's mask, but I still wore a chest protector and shinguards. It was no contest. He was just a little kid. He rammed into my knee — I tagged him — and he bounced off and fell back toward third base. He lay on his back in a cloud of dust, holding one hand over his eye. They had to take him out of the game. Within minutes, the eye was nearly swollen shut. You could see it was going to turn black. I felt bad about it, but I hadn't tried to hurt him. I was just doing what a catcher is supposed to do: I was blocking the plate.

I went two for four, and for my second hit I actually beat out a grounder to deep third base. I ran! And it felt okay. As a reward, I guess, Uncle Earl didn't give me any steal signs. He gave lots of take signs, though, to Kirsten and Geraldine. They obeyed him on their first at bat: Geraldine walked and Kirsten was called out on strikes. After that, they stopped checking for signs. And they each got hits. Geraldine's double drove in a run. Uncle Earl shouted from the coach's box: "Check the sign! Check the sign!" He never gave them a word of praise for getting hits. Anyway, they simply ignored him. Geraldine even stole a base — without getting a steal sign. As for the rest of the Worms, Danny pitched well, and our fielding wasn't too bad. We gave up four runs.

Unfortunately, we only scored three.

I knew Uncle Earl didn't like losing, but he seemed fairly calm after the game. His mustache never twitched. He told us to run four laps — one for each run they scored against us — and he went to the bleachers to talk to Mrs. Rule. I watched them talk as I ran. I was watching the Charm in his body language, and I was thinking how much nicer he was as a coach when he didn't place bets on the game.

My thoughts were interrupted by a voice at my side: "How's the giant salamander?" It was Kirsten, who had caught up with me on her fourth lap as I was running my third. She slowed down to keep pace with me. Actually, I wasn't running too slowly. Without pressing myself, without even thinking about it, I was keeping up with the end of the main group. My legs felt stronger. Or my body felt lighter. Or both. My pants, I'd noticed lately, were getting too short at the leg and too big at the waist.

"He's recuperating," I said. I couldn't look at her. "We had to amputate his leg."

"I'm sorry," Kirsten said.

We ran half a lap, side by side, in silence.

I wanted to say something. With every second that passed, it was harder and harder to break the silence. But with every step we took together, I felt more and more like speaking. I wished I had Charm.

Then again Kirsten said, "I'm sorry, Baba Beau Bo."

"You didn't really want him, did you?"

"No."

"I didn't really mean to give him to you, either."

Kirsten had now run all her laps but stayed with me, running an extra one.

All I'd wanted was for her to say she was sorry. And she had. Twice. Just as, I realized, I had apologized to her the other day. I didn't need to give her flowers. Or a salamander. Or a poem. Although giving things is *nice*. It just isn't *necessary*.

Now I looked at her. "I was trying to give you a poem."

Her eyes lit up. "You wrote a poem? Can I see it?"

She always lit up when the subject was poetry.

"I don't have it with me."

She smiled. All freckles. "Don't you bring your briefcase to baseball games?"

"Are you making fun of me?"

Her face got serious. "I would never make fun of you."

"It's at home."

"Let's meet later. You can show me the poem. And I have something I want to give you. You'll like it. I got it yesterday. My mother nearly had a fit when she saw it. If I don't give it to you soon, she'll —"

"Kirsten."

"What?"

"What does your mother have to do with it?"

"What do you mean?"

"Do you — I mean am I just — I mean —" I struggled for the words. I wasn't used to feeling tongue-tied. Before I could recover, the run was over. Immediately, Kirsten's mother took her by the shoulder and headed her toward the silver Buick station wagon. Mrs. Kohler looked upset about something.

Everyone else went home. Uncle Earl was still talking to Mrs. Rule in the bleachers. Sitting in the Coupe De Ville, feet on the dashboard, I changed the words to my song:

Time to go,
Baba Beau Bo,
See you at baseball practice.
Time to run,
Move your bun,
I like you and that's a fact, miss.

Kirsten called. My mother handed me the phone with a significant look in her eye. It was the first time a girl had ever called me.

Kirsten said she had something she wanted to give me. She didn't think I should come to her house just now because her mother was "in kind of a state." Could I meet her at the lake?

Of course.

Would I bring the poem I'd written?

Uh. Okay.

Instead of walking, I ran down to the lake — the short way. Kirsten was already there. She must have run, too. I watched her turn two cartwheels, then lean over backwards, land on her hands, and kick up her feet. It looked as if she had somehow turned herself inside out. And then she sprang upright on her feet.

"You're good," I said.

"Not really," she said. "I used to be on a gymnastics team, but I had to quit. I kept injuring myself."

"So what's bugging your mother?"

"You."

"What did I do?"

"Well. She's mad that you tripped her."

"That was an *accident*."

"I know, but she thinks you're . . . too rough. Like in the baseball game today when you clobbered that kid at home plate."

"I didn't clobber him. He ran into me."

"And last week when you knocked out that kid at third base when you were trying to steal."

"That was an *accident*. We had a collision. That's all."

"And . . ." Kirsten lowered her eyes.

"What?"

"The way we met."

"What about it?"

Kirsten looked up again. "Well, my mother asked how we met, so I told her how I was doing handsprings down at the lake. Right here. And you . . ."

It seemed so long ago. "And I what?"

"You sat on me."

"You told her *that*?"

"Well, it's true, isn't it?"

"Yeah but . . . you didn't have to say it."

"She asked."

"But you could've said you met me when I was feeding ducks. And you were doing handsprings at the same place. That would've been enough. But you *told* her. You *wanted* her to know."

"No. I just didn't care if she knew. I didn't think she'd go bananas."

"But she did."

"Are you mad at me?"

"Yes. No. I don't know."

"Are you going to sit on me?"

"*Of course not!*"

"Just kidding." She smiled, looking up at me. It was a tentative, questioning sort of a smile.

I couldn't help it. I smiled back.

Kirsten picked up a package about the size of a shoe box that was lying on the ground. She cradled it in both her hands. "Here. This is for you." It was gift-wrapped, but there were holes punched in the wrapping. "Careful! It's alive."

Cautiously, I peeled the gift wrap. Inside was a brown box with holes. Dark in there. Something scuttling.

"Open the lid a crack. But be careful. Don't let it out."

I lifted the lid. And there without any fear, standing at its full height on furry brown legs, meeting my gaze with eight little black eyes, snapping two front claws at me like castanets, was a gorgeous big-as-a-tennis-ball tarantula!

"You like it?"

"I *love* it." Suddenly I felt hot. I'd done it. I'd

used the L-word. Of course, I was talking about a tarantula. "Where'd you get it?"

"My cousin. His father made him get rid of it."

I closed the box. "Thank you. This is gorgeous. Does it have a name?"

"No. It's a she."

"Harriet," I said.

"My cousin says the females can live twenty or thirty years."

Would I still have Harriet when I was thirty-three years old? Or forty-three? Would she be the family pet? Would my children feed her, and watch her, and grow up with her, and miss her when they left home and started families of their own? Maybe I could breed her. Find a male named Tubman. Maybe Harriet Tubman's children could belong to my children and go on down the generations.

"Where's your briefcase?"

"I didn't bring it."

"You didn't? *You?* Without a briefcase?"

"I ran down here. I didn't want it banging."

She pursed her lips, grinning. "Something's changing."

Something was.

"But did you bring your poem?"

Suddenly I felt nervous. It probably was a lousy poem. Maybe it was too personal. What was I doing writing poetry, anyway?

She read with pursed lips.

She seemed to be reading it over and over again. What was she thinking? Maybe she could tell that my secret wish has always been to soar over trees like a dragonfly. That I hate being fat. That I don't want to be different. I don't try. I just am.

She must have read it ten times. Then she looked up at me and grinned. "I'm going to turn it into a song."

I froze. "Don't you *dare*."

"Just kidding. Have you showed it to the band?"

"No."

"Going to?"

"No."

"Are you quitting the band?"

"No." It had never occurred to me. But of course, now it had. "Not yet," I added.

"Want to be a duo?"

"You play music?"

"Piano."

I looked in those blue eyes. "Yes. We could be a duo. Let's try it sometime."

"Okay. Sometime." She smiled. "When my mother settles down."

And I suspected that without intending to, I had once again chosen sides.

GROUNDED

Sunday morning I ran. I took the long route down to the lake and then ran farther uphill. It was getting easier.

Passing Boone's house, his dog came out and ran alongside me for a while. Boone, on his deck, shouted, "Go, Babcock, go!" From the sound of it, you couldn't tell whether he was making fun of me or encouraging me. Knowing Boone, though, he didn't make fun of people.

Passing Dylan's house, I saw him getting in his car with his father, both dressed for church. Dylan, the cool cat in shades, finger-snapper, rock and roller, was Catholic. He went to Mass every Sunday.

I was no longer angry with Dylan. Dylan was Dylan. You had to accept him for what he was. And wasn't.

When he saw me, he waved — not with an open hand but a closed fist, the Black Power sign. I gave it in return.

Dylan was big on signs. I wasn't.

On a street corner, Danny was leaning against a stop sign, talking with Geraldine. Suddenly they started wrestling. It was playful, but it was wrestling. Then just as suddenly, they stopped and stared at each other, grinning.

This was my town; these were my friends; the sun was warm; the sky was blue; the air smelled of redwood; running made me strong; life was *good*.

Returning home, I found my father and mother at the table drinking coffee and trying to read the Sunday paper, but they couldn't because Uncle Earl was talking. He was goofy in love. He was telling all about Mrs. Rule — whom he called Rosemary. Rosemary has a Macintosh computer. Rosemary thinks fluorescent light is bad for the brain. Rosemary reads *The New York Times*. Rosemary likes okra.

Rosemary has a mole on her left cheek that first appeared the same day that she lost a tooth in third grade. Rosemary recycles Styrofoam. Rosemary can recite poems by Langston Hughes, sonnets by Shakespeare, and psalms by God.

"And what does Rosemary know about you, Earl?" my mother asked.

"Everything. I tell her everything."

"Does she know you're going to marry her?"

"Not yet."

"Shall we invite her to come to our house for dinner?"

"Yes. Wonderful. Perfect." Then suddenly a look of worry came to his face as he glanced over at me. "But *you*, Bodacious one, must be on your good behavior."

Me? What could I do to cause trouble? He acted as if *I* was the oddball of the family.

Next day as evening came I heard the sound of the MG pulling into the driveway. Through my bedroom window I could see my father park in front of the garage.

I met him walking into the kitchen. My mother was stirring a pot that was simmering on the stove. "You got mail," she said.

My father saw a large JiffyPak envelope on the table. His eyes got wide. He ripped it open and removed what I recognized as a bunch of his drawings. He read the letter that came with them, and his eyes narrowed into a frown. The frown deepened into a scowl. He slammed the letter down on the table.

"I'm angry," my father said.

My mother looked nonchalant, but — out of habit — she said, "Now, Thomas. Don't have a heart attack."

"I'm *really* angry."

For my father, it was a violent statement.

Now my mother looked surprised.

My father said, "They couldn't have even *looked* at these drawings."

My father reached for his pipe, his matches, his tobacco.

I said, "I thought you were going to try to sell it to the local paper. To establish yourself."

My father lit his pipe. He was calming down. He shook out the match and said, "This *was* the local paper. And I guess I established myself, all right."

Kirsten was waiting for me at school. She had a grim look on her face. "I'm grounded," she said.

"What for?"

"My mother. She found out about Sunday."

"What about Sunday?"

"I met you at the lake. You know? When I gave you Harriet."

"So?"

"I wasn't supposed to meet you."

"Why not?"

"I just wasn't."

"How'd she know anyway? Did you tell her?"

"No. But it's a public place. People drive by. Somebody told her."

"Why are people talking about us?"

Kirsten didn't answer. She just looked at me with an unblinking, level stare.

I said, "Why weren't you supposed to meet me at the lake?"

"I'm not supposed to meet you anywhere. I'm not supposed to talk to you."

And there in the schoolyard we stood, she and I, watched by our friends and maybe some enemies, too. I thought of the many differences between her and me — between our houses — our families. A mother who liked palm trees. An uncle who sometimes had to absquatulate. Acres of kitchen counter. A kitchen table littered with comic strips. I looked at those level blue eyes. What did she see when she looked at me? Nappy hair? Ashy elbows?

For just that moment, she seemed so very white. And I felt so very black.

"Your mother. When she says I'm 'too rough.' Is that a code word? Does she mean something else?"

Again, that level stare. "I don't think so." Clenching her jaw. "She can't stop us, though. She can't control who I talk to at school." Kirsten made fists with both her hands. "She's such a *bitch*."

At just that moment, I could have fallen into hate. I could have fallen into *blame*. I could have fallen into name-calling, into a lot of useless feelings. I closed my eyes.

I didn't want to fall.

I wanted to rise.

I opened my eyes. "It's all a misunderstanding," I said.

"What do you mean?"

"I can't explain."

Kirsten grabbed my right hand and held it between both of hers. Something odd happened. Something I couldn't describe. Something in the feeling of the moment that I will remember for the rest of my life. She stared me in the face with a look that was so intense, so fierce with meaning that I couldn't say a word. My body and mind felt strange forces realigning — family ties loosening, new bonds forming — as if suddenly the force of gravity had shifted and now the most important pull in the world wasn't my family or hers. It was us.

"If you can't explain it," she said, "I bet you can write a song about it." She let go of my hand.

I knew she was right.

How did she understand the inner working of my mind?

I stepped into my first class of the day feeling as if I was walking on an entirely different planet.

THE DUO

We had to forfeit our next baseball game. Dylan had the flu and with Kirsten grounded, we could only put eight Worms on the field. Uncle Earl didn't seem upset — without baseball, he could spend the day with Mrs. Rule.

I spent the day at home — until Kirsten called.

"Want to come over?" she asked.

"To your *house?* Are you *crazy?*"

"I'm all alone. My mother won't be back for a couple of hours."

"What if someone sees me?"

"Come the back way. Up the hill to the back door."

"But — Kirsten —"

"Don't you want to be a duo?"

"Yeah but —"

"Well, this is where the piano is. I can't exactly take it somewhere else."

I didn't try to bring my guitar. I simply brought myself — and my briefcase full of songs — to her back door.

The piano was in its own separate room. Not exactly a music room, it was more like a storage locker. There were boxes in a pile, a painting in a broken frame, skis, a couple of lampshades without lamps, some leather suitcases.

Kirsten sat at the piano bench. "Whatcha got?"

"All my songs."

"Let's try one."

"Most of them don't have music. Just words."

Kirsten played a couple of chords. "Let's put one to music."

I opened the briefcase and pulled out a sheet where I'd written:

Mama dear
Don't come near
The time has come that we parted.
Baby girl

Now a pearl
Will finish what you started.

Kirsten liked the sound of it. She played some notes, shook her head, then played some different ones.

"You can change the words if you want."

"No no. They're perfect. Try this." She played a new tune.

And so we worked. She wouldn't let me change a word. With a little help from me, though, she made up two more verses:

Mama dear
Life is queer
Not at all what you planned.
He ain't rough
But he's tough
And with him I will stand.

You can't stop me
He won't drop me
Some things are beyond your control.
My time to run
Yours is done
The young take the place of the old.

Next we moved on to a rolling boogie-woogie beat that didn't go with any of my songs but that Kirsten loved to play — and it sounded great on the piano — so I started calling out any goofy set of words that came to my mind as she hit the keys, reaching for rhymes like:

Took my dog on a walk to the park,
He asked me why the flowers don't bark.

Sat down to write my love a letter,
The pen said, "Can't you do any better?"

Went to the store and bought me a turtle,
The store man said, "Don't you hurt her."

Got a tarantula from my cousin,
He lives up north where the land is fruzzin.

Bought me a car called a Dynaflow
Paid the price marked on the doh.

Went to school with an orangutan,
Played great sports but didn't learn a thang.

In the school of the orangutan —

Suddenly Kirsten froze. The room was silent. "Did you hear something?" she asked.

"Do you think your mother's home?"

We both listened. There was no sound. Kirsten poked her head out the door where she could see through the front window to the palm trees and the driveway.

"No car," she said.

"Maybe I should go."

"Yeah. Maybe."

Neither of us moved. Neither of us spoke. Our eyes were locked. Then slowly, hesitatingly, Kirsten lifted one hand and gently touched my arm.

"It looks tight," she whispered. "Your skin looks so *tight*." She pushed a finger into the flesh of my arm. "But it isn't."

"What are you getting at?"

"It looks different. Stretched tight like the skin of a drum. Mine looks looser. See?" She pushed a finger into her own arm. The flesh gave, then it bounced back. Just like mine. "Yours looks tighter."

"Because I'm fat."

Kirsten shook her head. "You're not fat. Not really. Not anymore. You're *big*. You're the big type. Big frame. Big muscles. Must be all the vegetables."

"I've been running."

"That, too."

I was looking at my arm. She was right. Somehow, the skin did look tighter than hers. I said, "Maybe the difference is the freckles."

"God. You're so *lucky*."

"You don't like freckles?"

"*No*. They're so *ugly*."

"That's silly, Kirsten. You shouldn't be ashamed of the color of your skin."

"I *hate* 'em. I wish I had *your* skin."

"If you hate them, why don't you get a real deep suntan? Then they wouldn't show."

"I don't tan. I just burn."

"Then stay out of the sun. Or use sunblock. Use one of those super sunblocks that —"

"Won't work. I could stay in a cave for the rest of my life and I'd still have freckles. I have freckles *everywhere*. There is no place where — like — I wear a one-piece bathing suit — always have — and I still have freckles on my *belly*. See?"

She lifted her jersey to expose her stomach.

I leaned forward. Sure enough. There were

little pale freckles sprinkled all over her belly. They made me think of buds just waiting for a touch of sunshine to bring them bursting forth into flowers.

I poked a finger into the flesh next to her belly button. Just like her arm the flesh gave way, then bounced back. When I removed the finger, it left a white circle, which took a few seconds to turn pink again.

"Kirsten! *What* are you *doing?*"

In the doorway, holding a plastic bag from The Gap, stood Mrs. Kohler. And there on the piano bench sat her daughter and me, contemplating Kirsten's pale freckled belly.

There was a moment of stunned silence.

It seemed to me that there was not a great deal that I could say in that situation. All I said was, "Good afternoon, Mrs. Kohler, ma'am. I was just leaving." I grabbed my briefcase and — in a word — absquatulated.

GONE TO THE ORANGUTAN

Kirsten did not come to school the next day. Or the next. I didn't see her running by the lake. There was no answer when I dialed her number. At her house there was no Buick in the driveway under the palm trees.

On the street I met one of the giggly girl-friends, who wasn't giggling now. She said, "I have a message for you from Kirsten. She says her mother enrolled her in a private school. A boarding school. She has to get permission before she can use the phone. So she called me to tell you. She says she'll write when she can. She said — she told me to say this — she said, 'I'm going to the school of the orangutan.'"

I felt as if I'd been kicked in the appendix.

I thought of the words Kirsten had sung: *You can't stop me. He won't drop me. Some things are beyond your control.* It appeared that a few things were still firmly in Mrs. Kohler's grip.

Would I ever see Kirsten again? At least I should get to say good-bye. I felt a hollowness in the pit of my stomach behind my appendix, or above it, or wherever. Was this what a broken heart felt like? And if it was my heart, why did I feel it in my stomach?

So I ran. I didn't think about it. I just started running. I followed the path that Kirsten always took toward the reservoir. I made it about three-fourths of the way up the hill, then had to walk. Coming back down, I ran all the way. I wanted to howl at a lonely moon. I wanted to lie down in a dark room and never get up. I wanted to take a chain saw to those palm trees and cram them up — well, never mind. I ran longer, faster, farther than I had ever run before. And then I came home to a house where nobody had time for a broken heart.

This was the night when Mrs. Rule was coming for dinner. I wasn't in any mood for it. I

went to my room and threw my briefcase as
hard as I could against the wall, so hard it rattled the shelves. My mother was cooking on all
four burners of the stove. My father straightened up all his drawings into one pile, swept
the floors, and set the table. Uncle Earl per-
formed a complete set of ablutions and then
chirped around the house like a nervous bird
getting in everyone's way until he turned his at-
tention to me.

"Beau. You ain't gonna wear *that* old shirt,
are you? I got a shirt you can wear. But first you
gotta take a shower. You're *sweaty*. Do some
ablutions, boy. And it's time to shave that face."

"I don't shave, sir."

"I *know*. That's the *problem*."

"I don't know how to shave, sir. I don't have
any —"

"I'll *show* you, boy. You can use my razor."

So I showered. And then I shaved for the first
time: I dabbed shaving cream over my entire
face with two holes for my eyes to look through,
and Uncle Earl snorted "You don't shave your
eyebrows. And your nose — the only hair on
your nose is on the *inside*. Just get that fuzzy little mustache. On me it looks debonair. On you
it looks like mildew." When I finished, my skin

felt a little raw, but you could actually see a difference. I smelled minty and fresh from the
shaving cream. I felt scrubbed, scraped, and
clean like never before. I put on Uncle Earl's
shirt with the button-down collar, and then he
handed me a necktie.

"What's that?" I said.

"Haven't you ever seen a necktie before?"

"Yeah but . . . for *dinner?*"

"For Rosemary," he said, and he showed me
how to tie a Windsor knot. He found my dress
shoes and buffed them until they gleamed.
Then he held me at arm's length and studied
me up and down. "Charming, Beau. You look
absolutely charming."

I didn't feel terrifically charming. I still had
that empty feeling in the pit of my stomach.

A car pulled into our driveway. Uncle Earl
rushed out and opened the door of the Toyota.

My parents said, "It's so nice to meet you,
Rosemary," and I said, "Hello, Mrs. Rule." I
couldn't call her Rosemary. Ever. For two years
I'd sat in her classroom. She was the best
teacher I'd ever had, and also the strictest. To
call her anything but Mrs. Rule would be disrespectful. Even if she married Uncle Earl and

took his name, she would still be — always — Mrs. Rule.

Mrs. Rule had a problem with my name, too. She said, "Hello, Buh — uh, hello, there." She'd gotten used to calling me Babcock, as everyone does, but suddenly she sensed that it would be wrong, disrespectful, to call me that in front of my parents.

My parents knew what she was thinking.

"Go ahead and call him Babcock," my father said. "It's his one and only name. And it's our cross to bear."

"So it's true?" Mrs. Rule asked. "You really did let him choose his own name?"

"Isn't it amazing," my father said, "the mistakes we make when we're young?"

"And when we're not so young," Mrs. Rule said, looking directly at Uncle Earl.

For some reason, Uncle Earl squirmed.

Mrs. Rule wanted to see my room. She'd heard about my animals when I was in her class. I told her there'd been a few changes. Uncle Earl followed, but his lip was twitching. It seemed as if Mrs. Rule was visiting me, not him. When I took Martin Luther Kingsnake out of the terrarium and he started twisting around Mrs. Rule's arms, Uncle Earl left the room.

At dinner Mrs. Rule asked me how I was doing in school this year. I said my grades were good.

"They'd *better* be," Mrs. Rule said.

My parents laughed, but I knew she wasn't kidding. It occurred to me that if she married Uncle Earl, it would be like having her for my teacher — for better and for worse — for the rest of my life.

"Tell me, Beau," Uncle Earl said, "what's the worst grade you ever got?"

"C, sir."

"In what subject?"

"English, sir."

"Wouldn't you know it?" Uncle Earl put down his fork. He looked set to make a speech. I had a feeling he'd prepared it in advance, hoping to impress Mrs. Rule. "It's discrimination. Don't you think so, Rosemary? All those white teachers. I mean they ain't bigots, but they don't understand. If you speak with an African-American style, they think it's *wrong*. And then they use standardized tests written by white people. If we had more teachers like you, Rosemary —"

"If you had more teachers like me," Mrs. Rule said, "he'd get more C's. Until he learned where to put a comma. Which he did." She took on her in-front-of-the-class look. "I gave him that C. I guess I always did discriminate against people who won't learn punctuation."

Uncle Earl wore a sheepish smile.

In some ways, I still knew Mrs. Rule better than Uncle Earl did. She was the one who taught me about Frederick Douglass, Marcus Garvey, Sojourner Truth. She taught me never to feel sorry for myself. And she was a perfect example of what she taught — almost, I thought, too perfect.

"But you know, Earl," Mrs. Rule said, "what you were saying — it *is* a problem sometimes."

Uncle Earl sighed with relief. I knew the feeling, like when you're finished at the blackboard: *Good job, Earl. You may go back to your desk.* Why would he want to marry a schoolteacher?

My mother noticed that I wasn't eating. "Is something the matter, Baba?"

"I'm not hungry."

"Were you snacking?"

"No, ma'am."

"Do you feel all right?"

"I'm not sick. It's my stomach. It feels . . . funny."

"It's not your stomach," Uncle Earl said. "It's your heart."

My mother looked alarmed. "What's the matter with his heart?"

"I think it's broken," Uncle Earl said.

I wondered how Uncle Earl could always tell what was happening between Kirsten and me just by looking at my face. Maybe he *was* an expert on love.

"Did you try flowers, Beau?" Uncle Earl asked.

"This goes *way* beyond flowers!" I slammed my hand down on the table. At the same time, I thought I heard a crash from another part of the house, like an echo of my hand. "Don't *talk* to me about flowers."

"Baba," my mother said, "what is the matter?"

"She's been sent to a *boarding* school."

"Who?"

"Kirsten. You don't know her."

"Is she the girl who called the other day?"

"Yes."

"And you . . . *like* this girl?"

"Yes. I like her."

"Does she like you?"

"Yes, ma'am."

Uncle Earl waggled a fork at me and said, "I told you this would happen. I warned you about species. It's a matter of science."

"Would you *shut up*, sir?"

"Baba! Apologize to your uncle."

"I'm sorry. Sir."

"Boarding school, Baba? Species? Flowers? Would you mind explaining a little bit?"

So I tried: I told how we seemed to share the same interests — or grow into the other person's interests — like that I'd started running and she'd become a vegetarian, or how she liked poetry and I liked songs and now I'd written a poem and she'd written a song. I tried to explain how she and her mother were like nitro and glycerin sometimes and could blow up over some trivial thing, how her mother tried to chaperone Kirsten even when she was running. I said her mother thought I was too rough, how I'd accidentally knocked her over while I was rescuing Malcolm, how she'd seen me collide with kids in baseball games, how Kirsten had told her that I'd sat on her. And then I told how she'd come home and found me with my finger on Kirsten's belly.

"She was grounded?" my mother asked. "And you knew that? And you went over anyway?"

"Yes, ma'am."

"And you were alone in her house with her?"

"Yes, ma'am."

"And she took off her shirt?"

"No, ma'am. She just pulled it up. You see, we were talking about freckles. She was showing me that she had freckles on her —"

"Never *mind*," my mother slashed the air with her hand. "Maybe *you* should be grounded, too."

I looked around the table. My father hadn't said a word. He was leaning back in his chair with his arms folded across his chest. Mrs. Rule was sitting up straight — as always — and listening intently. Now she said, "Excuse me. I don't want to intrude on a private matter. But could you explain what species has to do with this? How it's a matter of science?"

So I told her that Uncle Earl warned me that blond people were a different species.

"What does that *mean?*" Mrs. Rule asked.

"That they don't mate with other people, ma'am. People who aren't blond."

"You'd *better* not mate," Mrs. Rule said. "You're too young for that." She turned to my father and mother. "Forgive me," she said. "I don't mean to intrude. Sometimes I forget that

I'm not in a classroom." Then she turned to Uncle Earl. "Of all the racist garbage I have ever heard —"

"Now, Rosemary, I was only joking."

"How would you like it if somebody told you —"

Mrs. Rule stopped in midsentence. Uncle Earl's lip was twitching as if it was attached to an electric wire. We all stared at him. Suddenly he jumped out of his chair and ran to a corner of the kitchen. "Get it!" he said in a high-pitched voice. "Get that thing!"

The thing was Harriet. She had climbed onto the table and was advancing toward Uncle Earl's plate when she stopped to explore a glass of ice water. With two furry legs, she touched the sweat on the outside of the glass.

I looked toward my open bedroom door. Hobbling on three legs, Malcolm was limping toward me across the carpet.

I ran to my room. Oh man! The noise I had heard earlier was the sound of my shelf falling over. When I'd thrown my briefcase against the wall, I must have hit the shelf support and weakened it, and it just gave out, and in falling it knocked open the door to the mouse cage and spilled the terrariums onto their sides. The fish-tank and jars of larvae fortunately were on the windowsill, untouched. On the loose in the house were one snake, one lizard, one horned toad, two mice, one Pacific giant salamander, and one tarantula.

From the kitchen I heard Uncle Earl screaming. I heard my mother saying, "Thomas! Don't have a heart attack." I heard my father incapacitated by laughter. I heard chair legs scraping and Mrs. Rule saying, "Do you have a jar? A box? Give me anything."

I scooped up Marcus, the horned toad of the living dead, who hadn't run anywhere, set his terrarium upright, and dropped him inside. I saw Douglass the white-footed mouse cowering under the bed. Caught him. Blue-bellied Garvey lizard was doing push-ups on my pillow. Got him. Malcolm and Frederick were not in sight.

I raced back to the kitchen. Mrs. Rule had dropped a wastebasket over Harriet and was just reaching over to pick up Malcolm. Malcolm raised his head and barked at her. *Ahack! Ahack!* She jerked her hands back.

"He won't bite." I picked him up. "He just barks."

"Like a watchdog, huh?" Mrs. Rule said. "You should post a sign in front of your house: BE-WARE OF SALAMANDER."

"And tarantula," my father croaked out be-tween spasms of laughter.

Mrs. Rule got down on her hands and knees with me on my bedroom floor, and between the two of us we found Martin Luther where he had slithered under a corner of the rug. But we didn't catch Frederick. We couldn't catch him because Martin Luther had caught him first — and put him in a place where no one would ever pet him again.

When we returned to the table, Uncle Earl was nowhere to be found. We called his name. I checked the bathroom. My mother checked the bedroom. My father checked the broom closet.

The phone rang.

My mother answered. "Where *are* you?" She turned to us. "He's in the garage." Into the phone she said, "Yes, Earl. It's safe to come back. Yes. It's time for dessert."

My father looked at me and winked. "Thank you, son," he said.

"What for?"

My father spread his arms as if he wanted to

embrace the whole room. "Stories of romance," he said. "Scenes of action. Violence. Treachery. Death. Tonight I've had it all."

I knew he couldn't wait to start drawing.

That night I lay in bed surrounded by scuffling sounds from my zoo — minus the scuffling of one mouse. From the kitchen I heard the rustling of paper and squeak of chair.

The hollowness was still there in the pit of my stomach.

LETTERS

After school, I found I had a piece of mail. Kirsten. I ripped open the envelope and found:

In the school of the orangutan
The desks are made of mud
The teachers throw the spitballs
They hit you with a thud.

In the school of the orangutan
You work like a computer
A little lady guards your room
Armed with a peashooter.

In the school of the orangutan
The headmistress wears a jock
You sit upon a battery
Wrong answers get a shock.

In the school of the orangutan
They tie your feet with chain
They nail your hands to heavy books
And microwave your brain.

In the school of the orangutan
The only food is meat
On clipboards they write what you eat
And how much you excrete.

In the school of the orangutan
Each day new kids arrive
The buses go home empty
No one gets out alive.

Signed: K.

I wanted to move. Run. Somewhere, I knew, Kirsten was running, too.

Quickly I changed my clothes and then set off jogging down the road to the lake.

Mrs. Kohler ran by.

So. She didn't run just because she wanted to chaperone Kirsten. She was wearing the purple sweatsuit with the purple headband.

Our eyes met.

I nodded.

I didn't smile; I didn't wave — that would have been too friendly for the way I felt about her. But also I didn't scowl at her; I didn't flip her off — that would have been stupid. I nodded as if to say: *You're a human being; I'm a human being; we owe each other a greeting.*

She stared at me for a few seconds, and then she turned her eyes forward and ran on by.

I stopped.

I turned and watched as she headed onto the trail that led to the reservoir.

Then I ran — after her — on the trail to the reservoir.

Mrs. Kohler must have heard my footsteps, though I was pretty far behind her. She looked back once, then kept on going. It occurred to me that she might be frightened to see me following her into the woods. If I had to name the emotion on her face when she looked back at me, it would be fear. But I only saw it for a second from a distance. She could also be angry at me for following her. Angry at me for a lot of things, as a matter of fact. But she didn't look back again, and she didn't change her pace.

I made it running all the way to the reservoir for the first time — but I couldn't take another step. Mrs. Kohler kept on running in a circle around the reservoir while I stood by some cattails, heaving for air.

Mrs. Kohler finished her circuit. She started back down the trail.

I started running again. Now, I was closer behind her. She never looked back, and I never caught up until we came out of the woods at the bottom of the trail. She slowed to a walk. I ran a few extra steps and came up beside her, though I kept the width of the road between us. Then I, too, slowed to a walk. I didn't look at her. We were both breathing hard. We walked past the lake. I didn't say a word. I had the feeling that something had to happen between Mrs. Kohler and me. Something had to connect. Or discharge. I wondered if Mrs. Kohler was going to start shouting at me now as she had shouted at Kirsten the other day. I wondered if I would shout back. But she didn't say a word. She didn't look at me, either.

We came to the point where the road to her

house split off from the road to my house. I turned one way, Mrs. Kohler the other. We'd never said a word or exchanged a glance. I walked home as a flock of chickadees bustled in the trees over my head.

I still didn't know what I had expected to happen between Mrs. Kohler and me, but whatever it was, it hadn't taken place.

And then I realized: Because nothing had happened, something had.

I wrote a letter:

Dear Kirsten,

I'll get you out alive.
Keep running.
I have a plan.

The only problem being that I didn't know what the plan was. And then there was another problem: How do I close the letter? I didn't want to use the L-word. We'd never spoken it to each other. She hadn't used it after her poem. Finally I decided not to close it at all. I simply signed it: *B.*

Every morning the stack of drawings on the kitchen table was higher than the morning before. One morning, however, the stack was gone. And so was the Coupe De Ville.

"What do you think he's up to?" my father asked.

My mother shrugged. "Maybe he wants to show them to Rosemary."

"At seven o'clock in the morning?" My father looked worried. "I put a lot of work into those drawings."

"I'm sure he'll take good care of them," my mother said.

"He'd better."

"Now, Thomas, don't —"

"I won't."

After school I had another envelope waiting for me from Kirsten. Inside was a sheet of music with notes and chords written by hand over the first verse of "In the School of the Orangutan." Scribbled at the bottom in her curly handwriting was: "Go ahead. Show it to the band."

We had a practice scheduled for later that afternoon. I rushed to my guitar with the sheet of music — and left it there. First there was important business: running. I changed my clothes, went straight to the lake, and waited, warming up, jogging in place.

Mrs. Kohler ran into view wearing a blue sweatsuit and blue headband. She started up the forest trail.

I ran right behind her.

The trail was narrow, so we had to run single file. Neither of us said a word.

What was going through her mind? I remembered running beside Kirsten after the baseball game when she was trying to apologize about Malcolm, and how the longer we went without speaking, the harder it was to say anything, and the more I wanted to say it. But this was different. I didn't know what I wanted to say to Mrs. Kohler — if anything. And if she had anything to say to me, it certainly wouldn't be an apology.

But I knew that with each step we took on the trail together while nothing else happened, something did.

This time when we reached the reservoir, I felt strong enough to run the circle around it, following Mrs. Kohler. Then we ran back down the trail.

At one point a man came jogging up the trail toward us. When he first came into sight, Mrs.

Kohler immediately looked back. Maybe I was reading too much into it, but I thought she looked anxious. When she saw that I was there, she seemed reassured. As we passed the man, he waved. I said, "Howdy." And Mrs. Kohler just kept on running.

Was she scared of running in the woods? Then why did she live in San Puerco, where all the houses were surrounded by forest — except for the house under the palms?

At the bottom, we slowed to a walk past the lake, keeping the width of the pavement between us.

When our roads split, Mrs. Kohler turned to look through the invisible wall between us. Here it comes, I thought. She's going to tell me to get lost. To quit following her or she'll call the police. To not even *think* about her daughter.

My upper lip started to twitch. I didn't smile. I just let it twitch.

She had dark eyebrows, just like Kirsten. Same blonde hair, maybe a little darker. Her skin looked tough, like armor, with wrinkles gathering sweat and fine flecks of dirt.

After a moment of silent study, she spoke: "Until tomorrow?"

My lip relaxed.

"Yes, ma'am," I said. Nothing more. What was happening — by not happening — was far too important for me to mess it up with words.

She walked toward home. And so did I — to my garage where the band, and Uncle Earl, had started without me.

"Where you been?" Uncle Earl asked.

"Running, sir."

"Can't be." Uncle Earl shook his head. "Beauregard Bodacious don't run."

"Baba Beau Bo does, sir. I've got a new song."

Together, we picked out the notes.

"Not bad," Boone said.

"We could do something with it," Law said.

"The words sound like something Chuck Berry might've made up," Uncle Earl said.

"Cool," Dylan said.

We worked on the song. Improved it in places. I never told them who wrote it. They weren't ready for that.

THE DUKE OF BABCOCK

After band practice, I followed Uncle Earl back to the house. My father had arrived home from work and was pacing in the kitchen. My mother, watching my father, was looking worried.

"Where are my drawings, Earl?"

"At the *Chronicle*."

There was a moment of silence. Then all three of them were talking at once.

"You took my drawings to the — ?"

"Now, Thomas, don't have a —"

"I was just doing you a favor. You need —"

"I don't remember giving you permission to take those drawings anywhere. I don't even remember you *asking* permission to take —"

"Calm *down*, Thomas."

"You need a salesman, Brother-in-law. You've got the talent but what you need is the marketing. I know how to —"

"When I'm ready to show those drawings I'll —"

"When you're ready to show those drawings I'll be an old man in a wheelchair."

My father crossed his arms over his chest. He said, "I showed those drawings to a syndicate. Twice. And then I took them to the *Tribune*. And you're not in a wheelchair *yet*."

"But you didn't *sell* them." Uncle Earl moved on his feet as he talked. He waved his arms. It was a dance. It wasn't Charm, but it was effective. "Your trouble, Brother-in-Law, is you don't know how to *sell* yourself."

My father didn't move. He was a boulder. "Did they buy them?"

"No." Uncle Earl shuffled his feet.

"So you *lost* my drawings and you didn't even —"

"I didn't lose nothin'. I left them with the assistant. I told him he needed to put some new life into his comic page."

"I'm sure he appreciated your editorial advice, Earl."

"I'll be honest with you. He didn't want to talk to me. I'll admit it. He said they hate to add new comics because once they get started, they can never get rid of them. People get *attached* to them. He said the last time they dropped a comic strip, people wrote nasty letters and they even had a bomb threat."

"So what did you tell him, Earl?"

"I told him maybe he'd get a nasty letter if he *didn't* take your comic strip. Maybe he'd get a couple bomb threats, too."

My father put a hand over his eyes.

"I was only joking," Uncle Earl said.

"Great," my father said. Again, he folded his arms. "So now the newspaper thinks we're a bunch of jerks. And they've got my drawings. I'll have to do them all over again."

"He said he'd pass them on to his boss."

"I don't suppose you gave him an envelope to return them in? An envelope with my address written on it and postage already paid?"

"No."

"Did it ever occur to you to make copies of those drawings? And give him the copies?"

"That's a good idea. Next time, Brother-in-law, I'll make copies before I —"

"*Next time?* There won't *be* any next time! Don't *ever* take my drawings again!"

I had never seen my father so angry. In a way, though, it was reassuring. It showed that my mother didn't need to worry so much. He could be furious and not have a heart attack. Not even a flutter. Which just went to prove what I already knew: My father's heart wasn't some delicate thing. It was a force of nature.

I got another letter from Kirsten. Two poems. And then:

What's your plan? How will you get me out alive?

She signed it: *K.*

Again I waited by the lake. Mrs. Kohler appeared in a yellow sweatsuit with a yellow headband. I fell in behind her.

We didn't speak.

The only sounds were the thud of our footsteps and the puff of our breath. I doubt if I could have spoken, anyway. Running uphill was hard work. Bright wildflowers lined the trail. Shafts of sunlight pushed their way past the high branches of the redwood trees and fell like spotlights on white curls of steam rising from wet logs. Clumps of fern unrolled bright green shoots. Sweat dripped from my nose and fogged my glasses.

As we circled the reservoir, little gray frogs hopped away from our feet and peeped from the marsh grass. Dragonflies crackled and buzzed near our heads.

Coming down the trail, we startled three deer from a tiny meadow. They leaped and were gone among the trees.

When we reached the bottom, we walked past the lake, keeping to separate sides of the road, catching our breath.

Just before our roads split, Mrs. Kohler turned to me and, I thought, wanted to say something. But no words came. And I had no words to offer.

So we parted.

Nothing spoken. But again, something said.

It was Friday night. I kept thinking of Mrs. Kohler in the yellow sweatsuit turning to

me, the yellow sweatband soaking wet, her
eyes meeting mine and her voice almost find-
ing words. What words? What was her question?

And what was my answer?

I took a shower. Totally abluted — washed
from my hair to my toes. Shaved. Didn't need
it, but it felt right. Trimmed my finger- and toe-
nails with Uncle Earl's golden clipper. Brushed
my teeth, gargled with mouthwash, slapped
some lotion on my cheeks, swiped some Ban on
my armpits. Buttoned Uncle Earl's shirt and
tied the necktie the way he'd shown me. Picked
a dozen daisies, walked to the house under the
palm trees, rang the doorbell.

Mrs. Kohler looked alarmed when she opened
the door and saw me. In a flash I wondered if I
was going to blow it all.

"Good evening, ma'am." I held out the daisies.
"These are for you."

She didn't smile. She looked confused. But
she took the flowers. "Thank you." The door
was half open. She was inside, and I was out.

"I just wanted to tell you, ma'am, I won't be
running tomorrow. I have a baseball game. But
I'll run Sunday morning. I'd be pleased to have
you join me."

She nodded. She looked at the daisies in her hand. She said, "Thank you, Babcock. Maybe I will."

"Okay, ma'am. Good-bye."

"Good-bye."

She closed the door. And I walked home. My heart was beating wildly as if I'd just had a fight — stood up to a bully — won a battle in a war that had no enemies, only people.

THE BUNT SIGN AGAIN

It was spring and the nights were warm. The open window brought the smell of pollen and the wash of the breeze. I heard Uncle Earl come home at two-thirty in the morning. I heard his phone ring — I don't know what time — and ring again later on. Tossing in my bed, I decided that Uncle Earl must not care very much about baseball anymore if he could stay out late and then talk on the phone all night before a game.

But I was wrong. Uncle Earl cared. He didn't seem at all tired in the morning as we drove to the game. My father came, too.

The bar crowd was there — six-packs and all, at eight in the morning. They looked like they hadn't slept — or shaved — or changed their clothes. They seemed *very* interested in the outcome of the game. This time, though, they were rooting for the Worm Farm.

"Slime those suckers!"

"Crawl on 'em!"

"Make 'em eat dirt!"

"Make 'em *pay!*"

My father sat as far away from them as he could get. I looked for Mrs. Rule, but she didn't seem to be coming.

Uncle Earl announced that he was going to "shake up the lineup." He took our two best infielders, Boone and Dylan, and put them in right and left field. Danny, our best pitcher, would play center field. Instead of catching, I would play shortstop. And Geraldine would pitch.

Boone looked puzzled. Geraldine looked pleased. Danny looked suspicious. Danny had a father who would give you pretty good practice, if you needed it, for understanding the likes of an Uncle Earl.

We took the field. Geraldine warmed up. It was the first time any of us had seen her pitch.

Uncle Earl was assuming that because she was a girl, she couldn't throw — even though she'd been firing the ball in from right field. Her first warmup pitch was soft — so soft, it ran out of gas and bounced in front of the plate. Geraldine swung her arm in a circle to loosen it up. The next throw was a little harder — and six feet to the right of the catcher. With each pitch, she threw a little harder. And a little wilder. Meanwhile, the first baseman was throwing practice grounders to the infield. They went right between my legs. I'd never played shortstop before. In the outfield, Boone, Danny, and Dylan threw fly balls to each other and caught them with ease.

The first batter was about three and a half feet tall. You could have measured his strike zone with a pair of tweezers. Geraldine pulled her hat down into her big ball of hair, wound up, and let fly with a screamer of a fastball. It flew four feet over the batter's head.

"Ball one," the umpire said.

The batter looked nervously toward the mound. Geraldine pulled down her hat — her hair kept popping it up again — wound up, and threw another screamer. This time it hit home plate and bounced straight up in the air.

"Ball two."

The batter moved back to the outside edge of the batter's box. He was leaning away from the plate. Geraldine dug a little hole with her cleats in front of the mound. Then she pulled down her hat, wound up with a big leg kick, and let fly. The ball came straight at the batter's head. He dropped to the ground with his arms up — and the ball hit the bat. The batter lay in the batter's box. The ball dribbled out in front of the mound, where Geraldine picked it up and tossed to first base.

"One out," the umpire said.

The second batter stood outside the batter's box. The umpire told him he had to stand inside. Cautiously, the batter moved to the rear corner of the box, as far away from Geraldine as he could get. His bat couldn't even reach the plate. Geraldine pulled down her hat, wound up, and lobbed one that floated gently right down the middle.

"Strike one."

The batter edged closer to the plate. Geraldine threw a screamer that came right at his feet. He jumped. The ball bounced in the dirt, hit the backstop, then deflected straight back and hit the batter in the helmet.

The batter threw down his bat and started trotting to first base.

"Come back here," the umpire said.

"It *hit* him," the boy's coach said.

"It has to hit him before it hits the backstop," the umpire said. "Ball one."

The boy came back. He moved back to the far corner of the batter's box.

Geraldine lobbed another one right down the middle.

"Strike two."

Cautiously, the batter moved a little closer to home plate.

Geraldine heaved a fastball that was so far inside that it passed behind the batter's back. He fell forward onto home plate.

"Ball two."

Now the batter didn't know where to stand. He moved to the rear of the box and stood there, twitching.

Geraldine pulled down her hat.

The batter leaned back.

Geraldine wound up.

The batter hopped a little on his toes.

Geraldine let go. The batter flinched. The ball sailed softly across home plate. Too late, the batter swung.

"Strike three!"

The next batter was a big guy. He dug in with his cleats. You could see he wasn't going to be intimidated. Geraldine kicked her leg way up and served a fastball that went two feet outside. Ball one. The next pitch was a fastball in the dirt. Ball two. Geraldine did a little earthwork on the mound with her cleats. Then she leaned back and fired a fastball that came right over the plate, belt high. The big guy swung.

Wap! The ball whistled over my head — and right into Boone's glove, in left field.

In the dugout, Uncle Earl posted the new batting order. Instead of batting cleanup, I was batting ninth. Geraldine moved from ninth to cleanup. Boone, Dylan, and Danny moved from first, second, and third in the order to sixth, seventh, and eighth, trading places with our three weakest hitters.

As it turned out, their pitcher couldn't find the strike zone. He walked the first three batters. Geraldine came up with the bases loaded. She checked Uncle Earl for a sign. Normally, he always gave Geraldine the take sign. Not this time.

The first three pitches were balls. Again Geraldine checked for the sign. With a three and 0 count and the bases loaded, a take would be automatic. But Uncle Earl didn't give her the sign. She could swing away.

The pitch came a foot above her head. Geraldine swung anyway.

Crack!

She stood at the plate, watching the ball fly. There was no hurry to run. The ball flew over the left-field fence to the parking lot, hit the pavement, bounced high in the air, and came down with a *boink* on the roof of Uncle Earl's Coupe De Ville. There would be a new dent — not that you would notice.

The bar crowd cheered.

Uncle Earl had a twitch on his lip.

The other team switched pitchers. This kid had control, and he retired the side.

In the second inning, Geraldine hit three batters and walked two. One player hit a grounder that rolled between my legs. Whenever they got a player on base, they'd steal second and then third. Our catcher — who'd never caught before — could barely throw the ball back to the mound. He didn't have a prayer of throwing out a base runner, and they knew it. Besides, Geraldine threw enough wild pitches that they could just wait for one to get away, then take the next base. Two struck out, and one hit a fly ball to Danny. The game was tied.

It stayed tied into the sixth inning. We traded runs. Geraldine had her good innings and her bad ones. At the plate, we went hot and cold, too. Then in the top of the sixth, we gave up two runs. We came up in the bottom of the sixth, down nine to seven.

Two outs, two hits, and I came up. Boone was on third, Danny on second. The crowd was rooting for me.

Uncle Earl touched his chest: the take sign.

The first pitch came in just over the knees. Strike one.

I checked the sign. Again, Uncle Earl touched his chest.

The second pitch was a ball.

I kept checking the sign, and Uncle Earl kept touching his chest. The count went to three and two, and I'd never swung the bat. The bar crowd was stamping their feet in the stands. Once more, I checked the sign. Uncle Earl made sure I was watching.

And then he gave the bunt sign.

It was no accident, either. He rammed his finger in there and held it.

That did it. That was the last straw. I felt my

lip twitching. I tapped some dirt out of my cleats with the baseball bat. Then I stood ready at the plate with my undertaker smile.

The pitcher threw the baseball.

I swung.

Thwack!

And I ran. The ball fell in the gap between right and center. I ran around first and headed for second. Boone scored. I rounded second and headed for third. Danny scored. The throw came to third. I slid.

"Safe!" said the umpire.

I looked up at Uncle Earl and glared. He glared right back. "Thought you hated to run," he muttered.

"Used to," I said.

Now we were back to the top of the batting order, which meant our weakest hitter was at the plate. So far, he'd walked once and struck out three times. He'd never moved the bat off his shoulder.

If he struck out, we'd go into extra innings facing the strongest part of their lineup, followed by the worst of ours.

The pitcher threw a strike. A ball. Another strike. The bat never moved. The next pitch was outside. The catcher reached — but the ball bounced off the edge of his glove and rolled slowly away.

I broke for home.

The catcher whipped off his mask and looked around wildly for the ball. "There! It's right there!" the pitcher screamed as he ran toward the plate. I was charging down the base path. The catcher saw the ball. He lunged for it. The pitcher stood at the plate. The catcher tossed the ball. I slid. There was a cloud of dust.

For a moment the umpire was frozen, hands on knees. Then he sprang up.

"Safe!"

The team mobbed me. The crowd cheered. Uncle Earl kicked clods of dirt, threw his hat on the ground, and stomped on it.

We had to run nine laps while Uncle Earl dealt with the six-packers.

Driving home, we began with a half hour of seething silence from Uncle Earl. His breathing was heavy, as if he was short of breath. He was sweating, though the day was cool. Then the egurgitation began. Uncle Earl stopped on a pull-over after a hairpin turn and threw up onto some poison oak. He looked miserable.

"Earl," my father said, "let me drive."

To my surprise, he agreed.

Even with my father driving so that all Uncle Earl had to do was sit, he breathed hard as I would breathe after a six-mile run. He was still sweating.

"You all right, Earl?" my father asked.

"I be okay," he said, panting. "I just have a problem" — one breath, two breaths — *ah hew, ah hew* — "with people who don't" — *ah hew* — "follow signs."

That made me mad. I said, "You don't give a bunt sign with two out and two strikes. Not unless you want to lose the game."

Uncle Earl leaned his head back, breathing deeply. "There's worse things" — *ah hew* — "than losing a ball game."

"Right," I said. "A whole lot worse. Like betting against your own team. And trying to throw the game."

My father raised one hand off the steering wheel and wiggled his fingers at me, and I knew he wanted me to cool it.

Uncle Earl was breathing harder than ever.

My father said, "Where'd you get the money, Earl?"

"Borrowed it," Uncle Earl said between clenched teeth.

"You found a — as you call it — an investor?"

"I found" — *ah hew* — "the only friend" — *ah hew* — "I've got in this world." Breath. Breath. "And now I've got" — *ah hew* — "to tell her" — *ah hew* — "it's gone."

"And since, as you say, you tell her everything, did you tell her what the money was for?"

Uncle Earl glared daggers at my father. He didn't answer, and he didn't speak again for the rest of the trip. Gradually, his breathing calmed down. He was still sweaty, though.

When my father parked the car in front of the garage and Uncle Earl stepped out, he suddenly became short of breath again. Sweat was gathering in his mustache.

"You all right, Earl?" my father asked.

"I be fine." *Ah hew.* "Just need" — *ah hew* — "a little sleep" — *ah hew* — "is all."

"Maybe you'd better lie down."

"Maybe" — *ah hew* — "I will."

Uncle Earl walked slowly into the garage.

I watched him go and said to my father, "If I had to tell Mrs. Rule what he has to tell her, I'd be in a sweat, too."

My father stared after Uncle Earl. "So would I."

"Is he going to run away now?"

My father was still staring at the garage. "I don't know, son. This will be the test."

"The test of what?"

My father didn't answer.

"I hope he stays. I — I like him, actually."

"We all do, son."

THE ULTIMATE CLICHÉ

Walking into the house after the baseball game, I found a letter waiting for me. I took it to my room and read:

"Absence makes the heart grow fonder"
is one thing I could say,
but I hate
a cliché.

Rain streaks my window.
Leafbuds drip.
Earthworms ooze over the sidewalk,
get stomped by boots,

drown in puddles.
But to compare my mood
to the weather of the day
is probably
a cliché.

My roommate stares into the mirror
squeezing a pimple
talking about some guy
who gave her a bouquet.
Carnations.
What a cliché.

I wish we had a hurricane.
I wish we had an earthquake.
I wish a tidal wave would strike
and a volcano blew up right under the —
No. I got it.
I wish the school would burn
and the headmistress runs out
in a flaming negligee
while I go to a matinee
play croquet
a holiday
in Monterey . . .
Rhyming
is cliché.

I want you to respect me.
I want to be original
to knock you out
with thoughts heretofore unconceived
with words like "heretofore"
lyrics cherry
for Chuck Berry
more sinceare
than Shakespeare
enough rhymes
for the New York Thymes
with metaphorical features
for English teatures
a poem that explodes these walls
— this distance —
instead of this business
we've skirted around
never dared
(scared)
to utter
but I think it's time to say
the ultimate
cliché:
I love you,
Baba Beau Bo Babcock.
Do you love me?

THE ULTIMATE
ABSQUATULATION

I spent two hours in my room trying to write a letter to Kirsten, trying to answer her question. After two hours, this is what I had written:

Yes.

Through my window I saw Uncle Earl emerge from the garage and stagger to the house. I heard the shower running, but there was no singing, falsetto or otherwise. I heard him performing ablutions at the sink, and twice I heard him say "Ouch!" and curse his razor blade. I saw him stagger back to the garage wearing only a towel and return half an hour later with his necktie hanging loose like a noose from his neck and the buttons of his shirt misaligned. The handkerchief in his breast pocket drooped out damp and wrinkly like a sagging mushroom.

My father and mother had gone to a wedding. If something had to be done with Uncle Earl, then the job was mine. Was he planning to absquatulate? In the kitchen he was taking flowers from a vase on the table and wrapping them — sloppily — with paper towels and plastic wrap.

"Are you all right, Uncle Earl?"

"I be" — *ah hew* — "fine."

He was still sweaty. He was still short of breath. And instead of minty and fresh, he smelled like whiskey.

"Are you running away?"

"I am not" — *ah hew* — "what you think."

"What are you doing?"

"Bringing flowers" — *ah hew* — "to Rosemary."

He waved his hand — and struck the vase. Water poured onto the table and floor.

I fetched towels and wiped up the mess while Uncle Earl staggered out the door, flowers in hand.

I got the water under control and ran outside. Uncle Earl was pulling the door closed in the Coupe De Ville.

"Where are you going?" I said through the open window.

Uncle Earl started the motor. He placed both hands on the wheel. "I'm bringing" — *ah hew* — "flowers" — *ah hew* — "to Rosemary."

"You're drunk."

"I be" — *ah hew* — "in control."

Uncle Earl took two deep breaths, shifted to reverse, and suddenly roared backwards — straight into three empty garbage cans.

He stopped. I ran to the car, reached through the window, turned off the ignition, and pulled out the keys.

Uncle Earl leaned back in the seat, staring at me, looking more puzzled than angry, breathing hard. Sweat was dripping from his forehead into his eyebrows and down his nose.

"You can't drive."

"I've got" — *ah hew* — "to bring flowers" — *ah hew* — "to Rosemary."

"You can bring them later."

"I can?" He looked surprised.

"Yes. You can. Later. Right now you need — um — you need to rest. You look tired."

"Tired?"

"Yes. Tired."

"It hurts."

"What hurts?"

"Hurts."

"Where?"

"Hurts." *Ah hew.* "Tired."

He opened the door. He swung one leg out to the ground.

"Help."

"What?"

"Bodacious."

"*What?*"

"Help me out."

I lifted him by his armpits. He grabbed onto the door of the car and stood there, swaying slightly.

"Flowers." *Ah hew.* "Get the flowers."

I reached into the car and grabbed the bouquet.

Uncle Earl draped an arm over my shoulders and stumbled, walking with my help, back to the garage. I lowered him to the mattress on the floor.

He looked up at me and blew whiskey breath into my face and said, "Flowers."

I handed him the flowers. He held them on his chest. Water was seeping out onto his coat.

"Do you need a doctor?"

"No." *Ah hew.* "Just rest."

"Good idea. You stay there, sir. You need rest."

"I be fine." *Ah hew.* "And Beau?"

"Yes, sir?"

"Flowers" — *ah hew* — "for Rosemary."

"For Rosemary. Yes, sir."

"Thank you" — *ah hew* — "Bodacious."

I turned out the light and left him in the dark. When my parents came home, I told them what had happened.

"Do you still have the keys?" my father asked.

"Yes, sir. Do you think he needs a doctor?"

"I'll check on him."

Both my mother and father went to the garage and returned to report that we should leave him until morning. Then when he was rested — and sober — we could see if he needed more help.

"Was he resting?"

"He was sleeping like a babe," my father said. "And snoring like a bull."

Sunday morning, I stretched by the lake. A golden fog rose from the water, spreading the glow of the rising sun. The town was quiet. No cars rumbled along the roads. At my house, everyone slept. At the lake, the bugs and the redwing blackbirds were alert and flying about. The ducks were tilting in the water, bottoms up, feeding on whatever they found in the murk.

Mrs. Kohler appeared in her purple sweatsuit. This time when she saw me and I nodded, she nodded back. I fell in place behind her. As usual, we ran in silence. Then about halfway up the trail when we were in the darkest part of the woods, I heard Mrs. Kohler's voice: "You know, we all need protection."

It seemed an odd beginning to a conversation. But then, in a way, we'd already been conversing for days.

I said nothing. I wanted to be very careful what I communicated to this woman.

We ran another hundred yards or so, the only sound the thudding of our shoes and the huffing of our breath, and then she spoke again: "It isn't just Kirsten. You need protection. I need

it, too. A long time ago when I was your age I
was —"

She broke off.

We ran between a couple of giant rocks where
lizards often scuttle and then across a little
creek where I've found red-headed garter snakes
that are supposed to be an endangered species.

A minute later, she said, "Anyway, I appreci-
ate having a chaperone."

I remembered how Kirsten had thought that
I was exactly what her mother was chaperoning
against. And I probably was. But now, appar-
ently, I wasn't. I said nothing.

We ran the rest of the way to the reservoir in
silence. As we were circling it, again I heard her
voice: "She told me you talked to dragonflies.
She told me you were gifted that way."

"Actually, ma'am, I talk *at* them."

"But they come to you."

"Sometimes."

"That's a gift. They must sense that you're . . .
gentle."

"Maybe, ma'am."

"I guess I'm not as perceptive as a dragonfly. Somehow I failed to sense that. Before. I
fail to sense a lot of things. It isn't my . . . my
gift."

"Kirsten told me that you think everybody is gifted in some way."

"She did? Well, what do you know? Yes, I said that. But when I talk to her I never know what goes in and what doesn't."

"She has a gift. She writes poetry."

"She told me you're the one who writes poetry."

"Songs, ma'am."

"Didn't you write her a poem?"

"One. Yes."

"She told me you were writing songs together, too."

"Yes, ma'am. But she writes poems. She's good, too. At least, I think so."

"She never shows them to me. Sometimes she's so . . . secretive."

We ran on without talking. We headed back down the trail through the woods. Partway down, Mrs. Kohler said, "I miss her, you know."

Now I really had to be careful. All I said was: "Me, too."

"When I run like this, I feel somehow close to her," Mrs. Kohler said.

Again I said, "Me, too."

We spoke no more until the bottom of the hill. Walking by the lake, Mrs. Kohler said, "The

thing is, Kirsten needs protection from *herself.*
Don't take it personally. She's such a *willful*
child. That's why she needs . . . what she needs.
And that's why she'll stay where she is and finish out the school year. Next year . . . we'll see."

She looked at me then as if she was genuinely
interested in what my response might be. But I
could think of nothing to say. That is, if I said
one thing, I was afraid I would say everything.
So I said, "Yes, ma'am," which was the same as
saying nothing at all.

Then we separated.

Back home, my mother and father were drinking coffee and reading the Sunday paper. I went
straight to my room, took out the sheet of paper — the one word — that I'd spent two hours
writing, folded it, and put it in an envelope.
Then I went back to the kitchen and asked my
parents if they'd heard from Uncle Earl.

My mother frowned. "Somebody should check
on him. Make sure he's okay."

"I'll go." I was wondering what would happen between Uncle Earl and Mrs. Rule. How do
you tell somebody that the money you borrowed was lost on gambling? When she was angry in front of a class, her nose got bigger. Or

maybe it just seemed that way. How big would her nose get with Uncle Earl? Would he even notice? Maybe I should warn him to watch for it. I felt like an older brother ready to advise little brother Earl on how to handle a teacher I'd had. Uncle Earl had wanted me to call him Brother. Bro.

The main garage door was now a wall. I knocked on the side door. It had a half window. Uncle Earl didn't answer my tapping. With my hands to the glass to make shade, I tried to peer inside.

It was too dark in there.

I tried the doorknob. Unlocked. Swinging it open, I called softly: "Uncle Earl?"

No answer.

Uncle Earl was always noisy in his sleep. But now there wasn't a sound.

I walked inside. In the dim light I could see Law's drum set in the corner. I could see a five-gallon bucket and a roll of drywall joint tape. I could see a rope strung between two sides of the garage with Uncle Earl's clothes on hangers. I could see the mattress on the concrete floor, and Uncle Earl lying on top of the sheets, fully clothed, with the flowers still clutched in his hand. His eyes were open. His face was calm. One narrow beam of sunlight squeezed through a crack between the wall and the roof and fell upon the bouquet on his chest.

"Uncle Earl? Are you all right?"

He made no sound. His chest didn't rise or fall. His pants were stained.

I kneeled beside him and touched his hand. Stone-cold.

For a minute — two minutes — five minutes — I remained on my knees in that half-converted garage squeezing Uncle Earl's rubbery cold hand while I felt tears running down my cheeks, while I heard my heart racing, while motes of dust rose in the beam of sunlight, while a twisting river of ants flowed to and from a jellybean crushed on the concrete floor.

I wanted to sing falsetto. To dress with Charm. To give flowers to every angry woman in the world.

Then I walked to the kitchen to tell my mother and father: The Duke of Earl would never absquatulate again.

AS IS

A sheriff's deputy parked in our driveway and left his radio barking. Then an ambulance — a huge van full of medical equipment — came for Uncle Earl. I took the flowers off his chest. They lifted him onto a gurney, covered him with a sheet, and wheeled him away. Why did they need a fully equipped ambulance to pick up a dead body? Why do they always cover dead people's faces? Where were they taking him?

I held the flowers. They were wilting from a night without water.

My mother took it hard. Then she called Mrs.

Rule. She spent a half hour on the phone, and I could tell from what my mother was saying that Mrs. Rule was nearly hysterical. Working to calm Mrs. Rule down, my mother became calm herself. She invited Mrs. Rule to come to our house, and an hour later Mrs. Rule arrived, looking distraught. My mother hugged her.

I handed the flowers to Mrs. Rule.

She thanked me. She almost said my name, but she caught herself with a "Thank you, Buh — Uh, thank you." She still felt awkward calling me Babcock when my parents were around. After all, it was their name, too.

"They aren't from me," I said. "They're from Uncle Earl."

"What do you mean?"

"Last night — he sort of made me promise."

"Sort of?"

"I didn't understand it at the time. That I was promising."

"Promising? What sort of promise?"

"He said, 'Flowers for Rosemary.' I said, 'Yes, sir.' He said, 'Thank you.' It was the last thing he said."

"The *last* thing? Exactly that?"

"Well. Actually, he said, 'Thank you, Boda-cious.'"

Mrs. Rule held the flowers to her nose and breathed deeply. Then to my shock she hugged me. It seemed as if the brick walls of the school building itself had reached out and grabbed me — but this wall was warm, soft, and trembling with emotion. When she let go, she said, "Thank you. Thank you, Bodacious."

She straightened herself. With a tissue she wiped her eyes. And there before me was the Mrs. Rule of old, the Mrs. Rule who dominated a classroom, although holding Uncle Earl's bouquet. And I knew that the next time I saw her, she would show no sign that she had ever been hurt by anything in the world.

I also knew that when she found out what Uncle Earl had done with the money he had borrowed — if she ever asked, now — she would forgive him.

Uncle Earl was right about flowers. He was right about a lot of things.

My father asked me to go for a ride.

We took the MG.

Of course, it wouldn't start. My father opened the hood, fiddled with something, then got it going. Neither of us said a word about it. Business as usual with the MG: It needed special care, and whatever it needed, my father would give.

We drove with the top down and our elbows hanging over the doors. Spring air blew through our hair and whistled in our ears. The motor purred. All the world was green and flowering. The MG wasn't powerful; it wasn't fast; it wasn't sleek, or luxurious, or even comfortable. But it was fun. It was the perfect car for a drive through the mountains on a sunny day in the spring. The driver's seat was permanently in-dented with the shape of my father's body. As my father had grown larger, so had the indenta-tion. He'd bought the car before he'd met my mother, and he'd loved it all these years. It was part of the family. People were always pestering him, wanting to buy it. He always told them that selling the MG would be like selling one of his own children.

"They think he had a heart attack," my father said after a while. "They won't know for sure until they do an autopsy, but they said from what we told them, it sounded like a classic case."

"Uncle Earl told me he hurt. But he didn't say how."

"He may not have hurt real bad." My father shook his head. "Sometimes a heart attack doesn't hurt at all." He bit on his lip. "Mm. Mm. *Mm.*"

We drove on for a while, each of us lost in our separate thoughts. But then I had to ask, "If we'd taken him to an emergency room yesterday, could they have saved him?"

My father winced. "We'll never know, son. But don't blame yourself. He was confused. Not to mention *drunk*. And he told you he didn't want to see a doctor."

"Do you think he knew what was happening?"

"Maybe. Maybe not. You've got to remember, he wasn't thinking about his health. He was thinking about Rosemary. He was thinking he blew it big time."

I thought of the pain I'd felt in my stomach when I heard that Kirsten had been sent to a boarding school. Could Uncle Earl have mistaken a heart attack for a heartache?

By this time we had come down the mountain and were passing through an outlying suburb where rich people lived and horses grazed. My father slowed the MG down to twenty-five.

The police here loved to give speeding tickets to people who didn't live in their town.

I asked my father, "Do you think he wanted to die?"

"No." My father rubbed his chin. "Not exactly." He rubbed some more. "I think he was trying to turn a new leaf with Rosemary." He let go of his chin and shifted gears. "I think he came here — to us, to California — to start a new life. But he found that he was who he was, and you can't change yourself with a snap of the fingers. You are who you are. You can change — yes — but change comes slowly, and it comes with a lot of backsliding. And he couldn't handle the backsliding. I think maybe he felt like quitting, yesterday. I think that's why he was drunk. Drinking is a way of quitting. But did he want to die? I don't think so. And I know that if he'd lived, he would have tried again. Earl had too much spirit to stay down for long."

"He could fix wristwatches. He had tools. He could've made a living that way."

"Maybe." My father shifted gears. "Maybe not. It's such a quiet occupation. Earl needed — you know — something *brassy*."

By this time we had passed into another suburb and were driving along a six-lane highway
with fast food and gas stations and used-car
lots. I had never asked where we were going,
but I found out when my father pulled into a
parking lot next to a squat building between a
Safeway and a chiropractor's office. A small
sign read THE NEPTUNE SOCIETY.

I went in with my father and sat with him in
an office while he made the arrangements for
Uncle Earl to be cremated. As for what to do
with his ashes, they offered us a choice: An air-
plane could scatter his ashes over the mountains, or a boat could take them to be cast in the
ocean. My father turned to me and said, "I don't
think Earl was ever comfortable in the mountains, do you?"

"No, sir."

"We'll drop him in the ocean." My father
signed the papers and gave the man a credit
card. A minute later, the man said that the
charge was "declined." In other words, the
credit card was already charged up to the limit.
So my father wrote a check, and we went back
to the car.

The MG started after he fiddled under the
hood. We drove without talking for a while. My

father broke the silence when he said, "I just wrote a bad check."

He looked uneasy. I didn't know what to say.

"I wasn't planning on paying for a funeral this month," he continued. "We just paid the obstetrician in advance. And we had to pay a deposit at the hospital. The price of babies has gone up with inflation. It's not like when you were born."

"How much did I cost?"

"I don't remember." My father glanced at me and smiled. "But I think we got you on sale. Marked down. As is."

"Can't you get arrested for writing a bad check?"

"We'll cover it. Your mother will figure it out." He was trying to sound sure, but he didn't *look* sure.

"How will she figure it out? How do you pay for something if you don't have the money?"

"You use money that was supposed to pay your other bills."

"What happens if you don't pay your other bills?"

"They come and repossess what you bought."

"They'll repossess *Uncle Earl?*"

"No, son. Something else."

"Like what?"

"The house."

"So we'd be homeless?"

"Well. We'd be houseless."

"Why do we have to pay for the cremation? If we didn't pay, wouldn't they have to do something with his body, anyway? They can't *make* us pay, can they?"

"No. Probably not."

"Then why are *we* paying for it?"

"Because we're family. And because to not pay would be disrespectful."

"Do you ever worry about money?"

"I'm worried *right now* about money."

"Can we afford to have a baby?"

"You don't *afford* babies. You *have* babies. You want your mother to have an *abortion?*"

"No, sir." The thought chilled me.

As he was speaking, my father's eyes kept glancing down at the dashboard. Now he pulled to the side of the road, left the motor idling, and opened the hood. As he was probing and pulling at wires, the engine quit. He slammed the hood.

"Get out, son. Help me push."

"What's the matter?"

"Generator's broken. Battery's running down."

I pushed from the rear. My father pushed from the side. When it was rolling, he hopped in. There was a POP, and the engine started. He braked, and I climbed in.

I asked, "Will it keep running long enough to get us home?"

"We'll see."

"How much does a new generator cost?"

"I don't *know*. Would you *stop* asking so many —" He caught himself. "I'm sorry," he said.

"That's all right, sir." I didn't ask any more questions.

The battery never ran down. But we didn't make it home. About five miles from San Puerco, I heard a *clunk* followed by a growling sound from the motor, while a thick cloud of black smoke poured out of the tailpipe. My father immediately pulled to the shoulder, cut off the ignition, and buried his face in his hands on the steering wheel.

Two hawks soared overhead. From where we sat I could see a red barn set among hills that rolled on and on to the ocean.

My father lifted his head from his hands. Like

the car, he seemed broken. "Threw a rod," he said. He sat and stared out toward the barn and the rolling hills.

I hopped out of the MG and stood at the side of the road. For a couple of minutes, no cars went by. Then two cars came practically bumper to bumper, but I didn't know them. There was only one main road to San Puerco, and everybody in town broke down on it at one time or another. Since everybody in town knew almost everybody else, you could count on getting help. The third car to come along, a minute later, saw me and stopped. The driver was Carla, Danny's father's girlfriend. She gave us a ride back to our house. She was chatty, but my father only grunted. I tried to be sociable.

Once home, my father went straight to the telephone. I thought he was arranging for a tow truck, but a few minutes later he came into my room, sat down heavily on the bed, stared blankly at Sojourner and Truth circling mindlessly in the aquarium with their puckered goldfish lips, and told me the news: "I just sold the MG," he said. "Marked down. As is."

BROWN LEATHER SHOES

I could have stayed home from school. I could have "mourned" Uncle Earl, or stayed home "out of respect" for Uncle Earl, but the house was such a gloomy place right then, I couldn't stand it. And I didn't think that Uncle Earl — someone who couldn't even *sleep* quietly — would expect me to sit around grieving for him. If *he* were in my situation, he'd go to a bar and pump quarters into the jukebox.

I don't do bars. I do school.

After school I checked the mail and found my usual letter from Kirsten:

Sometimes
I get lonely
There's a piano I can play
So I sit here at the bench
Then I feel okay.

I pound out
Boogie-woogie
On this piano I can play
It helps me to remember
Things we used to say.

I'm writing
Another song
On this piano that I play
Music for two voices . . .
Yours, so far away.

My mother had stayed home from work. My father had gone to complete the sale of the MG and have it towed to the new owner. He drove the Cadillac. It wasn't his type of car, and he'd told my mother that as soon as we could get the paperwork straightened out, we'd get rid of it. But the pink slip was made out to Uncle Earl, so the paperwork might take months. In the meantime, the Cadillac — dents, rust, and ragged seats — would be his car.

I went to the lake to wait for Mrs. Kohler.

She never showed up.

I waited forty-five minutes, then ran by myself to the reservoir and back. I didn't have any arrangement to meet her, but still it troubled me that she hadn't appeared. Maybe she didn't want to see me. Maybe there was some new problem with Kirsten that she thought I'd caused. Maybe she regretted that she'd spoken to me yesterday.

I returned home where the Cadillac was now parked next to my mother's van in the driveway. My father and mother were in the kitchen, my mother cooking dinner, my father sitting morosely in a chair.

I went to the garage. I'm not sure why. One reason, I guess, was that I wanted to get away from the gloom of my father. He missed the MG. He was worried about money. And I think he did blame himself, at least partly, for not taking Uncle Earl to an emergency room, for not recognizing the sweating and shortness of breath as symptoms of a heart attack. And ever since Uncle Earl had taken his comic strip panels to the newspaper and left them there, he'd done very little drawing. He seemed overwhelmed by the idea of redrawing all the panels that he'd lost, and he didn't seem to have the willpower to go to the newspaper and ask to have them back.

But I could have stayed away from my father without going to the garage. I guess I was trying to face something there. It wasn't that I was facing death — nothing grand or courageous like that. I was facing *loss*. I was facing the fact that I was still there, the garage was still there, Uncle Earl's shoes were still on the floor and his clothes were still hanging on a rope . . . *everything* was still as it was. But Uncle Earl was gone. I'd lost a big brother. I loved him.

That word.

I sat on the edge of the mattress. His brown leather shoes gleamed in the dim light. Uncle Earl never wore jogging shoes or hightops or anything but genuine leather, and he kept them polished. I slipped off my sneakers. The brown leather shoes were just my size — well, almost — maybe half a size too large. Wearing them, I walked to the band's corner and picked up my guitar. Absentmindedly I started strumming chords without any electric pickup.

In brown leather shoes
Caught in the sticky
Web of history
In a high school gymnasium
Louisville, Kentucky
Keeping the backbeat
You can't lose it
Any old time you use it
Though it wasn't the high point
Of your life.
What was?

The phone rang. Uncle Earl's phone. I stopped playing. By now everyone in town knew he was dead. A junk call? I set down the guitar and answered on the fifth ring.

The voice — a woman — asked for Earl Jackson.

Was this another girlfriend? Had he been cheating on Mrs. Rule? Or was it an old girlfriend catching up with him? Did I have to be the one to tell her he was dead?

"He — uh — he's not here," I said. Which was the truth.

"I've been calling all day. Why don't you have an answering machine?"

"I — uh —"

"I would think that an agent wouldn't want to miss any calls."

Agent? Uncle Earl? "Uh. Yes, ma'am."

"Can you take a message?"

"Yes, ma'am."

"My name is Philippa Graham. I'm the features editor. He left some comics here. By a Thomas Babcock. You know what I'm talking about?"

"Yes, ma'am." Now I got it. Uncle Earl had represented himself to the newspaper as my father's agent. He was probably expecting to get a percentage of the profits, too. "Would you send them back? Please, ma'am? I know he forgot to give you a return envelope or postage, but —"

"Send them back? We want to *run* them. We want *more*. The characters are so real, I feel like I've *talked* to them."

I could have told her that she was talking to one at that moment, but instead I gave her the phone number of the house and told her that if she called right now, she could speak to the artist himself. The agency — *ahem* — would step out of the picture.

A few seconds later, I heard the phone ring in the house.

I stayed in the garage for a while longer. I

pushed Uncle Earl's mattress up against a wall, cleaned up some scraps of drywall and fiber-glass insulation, and generally straightened up for a band practice. It was time we got together again. Maybe tomorrow. We needed to get some gigs, make some money. We needed pub-licity. How would Uncle Earl do it? Make some posters:

TWO ONE FIVE FIVE TWO!
LIVE CONCERT!
SPECIAL GUEST STARS:
JIMI HENDRIX
JOHN LENNON
AND ELVIS!

Still wearing the brown leather shoes with the spit-and-polish shine, I picked up Uncle Earl's scuffed black briefcase and carried it to the house. My father was just hanging up the phone. On his face was a big, goofy grin.

In my room I set the briefcase down next to my own. My fingers were long, delicate, ready to learn.

CHARMING AND A LITTLE STRANGE

We were eating dinner. The phone rang. My father answered, listened, looking puzzled. He turned to my mother. "Do we want to accept the charges on a collect call from somebody named Kirsten Kohler?"

"*Yes!*" I shouted.

I leaped to the phone. My mother and father sat at the table, watching, making no secret that they were listening. Of course, they could only hear what I said, not what I heard.

"Hello?"

"Baba Beau!"

"Hi."

Pause. "That's all? Just 'Hi'?"

I squirmed. I felt my parents' eyes. "It's good to hear your voice," I said.

Pause. Then her voice: "I'm scared."

"What's the matter? Is it that school?"

"I'm not in the school. I ran away."

"How? Where are you? What do you mean?"

"I ran. Away. I just started running, and after I don't know how many miles I got on a bus, but I didn't have any money so I kind of argued with him — the driver — kind of pleaded, and he kept driving while I was talking but then he put me off, and now it's getting dark and there's these guys outside."

"Outside what?"

"The 7-Eleven."

"You're in a 7-Eleven?"

"Actually, I'm just outside the door. That's where the phone is. The guys are in the parking lot. There's this laundromat next door. I think they've got stuff in the dryer. They're looking at me. I may have to go back inside."

"What are they doing?"

"Nothing. Just being jerks. But I'm scared."

"Where's the 7-Eleven?"

"Highway One. A little north of Monterey."

She was about a two-hour drive from San Puerco.

"Kirsten, those guys —"

"They're going back. Inside the laundromat."

"What are you going to do?"

"I'm not scared anymore. They're just doing laundry."

"But what are you going to do?"

"That's why I called. You've got to come here. I'm not going back. In the School of the Orangutan, they serve you stale banana. I'm calling up my Baba Beau. We're going to Montana."

"Kirsten. Don't make jokes. This is serious. What are you going to do?"

My mother was leaning back in her chair, staring at me, listening. My father sat forward with his chin on his fists. I had a feeling that a new episode of his comic strip was unfolding in front of his eyes.

"I'm not joking," Kirsten said. "I'm not going back. Can't you meet me here? Or somewhere?"

"Kirsten. I can't drive."

"Get your uncle."

She didn't know he was dead. But she was right that if Uncle Earl was alive, I could turn to him. He'd rescue a damsel in distress. He'd speed down to Monterey and pluck her from the 7-Eleven. Without him, who could I turn to? My parents? Perhaps. But they'd have a lot of questions, and they might want to talk to . . .

Mrs. Kohler.

"Kirsten, you've got no money. I could get a little, but —"

"Good. Get it. We'll get work. We can hitch-hike or something. Won't it be great?"

"No."

Silence.

"Kirsten, it won't work."

More silence.

Finally she said, "So you won't help me?"

"Yes, I'll help you. I'll send — uh — somebody to get you."

"Your uncle?"

"No. Somebody else."

"Who?"

"You'll see."

"I'm not going back."

"No. Of course not. The — um — person will bring you here. To San Puerco."

"Good idea. I'll hide somewhere. We'll figure something out."

"Kirsten."

"What?"

"You won't have to hide."

"You've got a plan?"

"Yes. Go back inside. It'll take a couple hours to get down there. Are those guys still there? Are you safe?"

"I'm okay. They're folding towels. I'll be safe inside the store. There's a woman working at the counter. She looks okay. Baba Beau Bo! I knew you'd help."

We said good-bye. I hung up. My parents were still staring.

"What's the trouble?" my father asked, lifting his chin from his fists. "Can we help?"

"Stay by the phone. She might call again. I've gotta run. See somebody. Don't worry. I'll be back in a few minutes."

I ran to the house of the three palms.

I pushed on the doorbell.

Mrs. Kohler opened the door.

I was out of breath. "Excuse me, ma'am." I took three breaths.

"Is this an invitation to run?" she said. "I couldn't go this afternoon because —"

"No, ma'am." I gulped two breaths. "I just talked" — breath — "to Kirsten."

"She's not supposed to use the phone without —"

"She ran away."

Her eyes widened. Her nostrils flared. "Are you sure? The school hasn't — I haven't heard anything."

"She just called. She ran away" — breath — "and then she got on a bus and now she's" — breath — "at a 7-Eleven north of Monterey and she says" — breath — "she's not going back."

"Going back?"

"To school. She's not going back."

"But is she all right?"

"She's fine. But she *hates* that school."

"She's told me," Mrs. Kohler said in a flat voice.

"If she has to go back there, I think she'll do something dangerous."

"She's *already* done something dangerous. She's run away. She never thinks ahead. That's why —" Mrs. Kohler cut herself off.

I had to agree with Mrs. Kohler: Kirsten didn't think ahead. She was willful. And hotheaded. She needed protection — from herself. We only disagreed on who should protect her.

"She's waiting in the 7-Eleven," I said. "She needs somebody to pick her up. That's why she called me. I told her I'd find somebody."

"Somebody. Meaning me?"

"Yes, ma'am. But I didn't tell her that. I was afraid she might — uh — you know."

Mrs. Kohler nodded. "I know."

Mrs. Kohler looked at me with the same expression you see at the grocery store when someone is choosing among a pile of tomatoes: This one's too soft, this one's too hard — they've bred out all the flavor — pick 'em when they're still *green* — haul 'em around in *trucks* — cost too much — spray 'em with pesticides — oh what I'd give for a homegrown tomato — this one's too small, this one — squeeze — it'll have to do.

"She's so . . ." Her voice trailed off.

"Willful?" I suggested.

"Stubborn. Willful. Muleheaded. Misguided." Mrs. Kohler sighed. "And so am I."

I was tempted to say, *Yes, ma'am.* But I kept quiet.

"And," Mrs. Kohler said, "I love her so very much."

"So do I," I said.

Again Mrs. Kohler's eyes widened. She stared at me from head to toe.

I stood there, panting, gradually getting my breathing back to normal. A cool breeze dried my sweat. The palm trees swayed and rattled. A full moon floated over the trees. From the lake I could hear the distant quacking of ducks. A dog yowled. The air crackled with magic — with life — with the spark of a night in spring when anything could happen and anyone could fall in love. It was the kind of a night when cats go on the prowl, when music floats from an open window, when lovestruck possums waddle into the road and freeze in the headlights of cars.

"You are a charming young man," she said at last.

"Thank you, ma'am."

She shook her head. "Though I suspect," she added, "you are also a little strange."

"Yes, ma'am." I thought of my father's words: You are who you are.

"All right. I'm going."

"Yes, ma'am."

She turned and walked to a little table in the entryway where she picked up her purse.

"Mrs. Kohler?"

She looked straight my way.

"May I go with you?"

She grasped the purse. Her eyes were hard. My question was intrusive. My entire visit was intrusive. Kirsten's running away was intrusive. Youth — love — the magic air of the night — everything was intrusive on her orderly life beneath the three palms. Then her shoulders suddenly relaxed. Her face softened. She let out a long breath, and I realized she'd been holding it ever since I'd asked my question.

"No," she said.

"Where are you taking her?"

She breathed in — hard — and again she was holding her breath as she met my eyes. Then again, she relaxed.

"I'm bringing her home," she said. "If she calls you again, tell her I'm on my way."

THE GIFT

When I first saw Kirsten at school the next day, I felt a twisty sort of feeling pass from my head down to the pit of my stomach, a mixture of joy — and terror. Was she mad at me for sending her mother?

She walked toward me carrying a couple of books and wearing the bright blue backpack — filled with, I wondered, how many poems? Everyone was watching.

She stopped a foot away from me. She held the books in front of her. She didn't smile. "Baba Beau," she said.

"It's good to see you," I said, which was lame, but suddenly I was feeling big and awkward and stupid — and strangely nervous, as if I was on trial.

Kirsten frowned. She looked up at me and said, "When I saw that silver Buick pull into the parking lot at the 7-Eleven, I tried to hide. I tried to run out the back door. I was *mad.*"

"Well, you see, Kirsten, I was afraid if I told you that your mother was coming you'd —"

"I thought you'd turned me in."

"Well. I know it may seem that way but —"

"You were right, too. I would've — I don't know what I would've done. Something stupid."

"You're not stupid."

"No. But I can do stupid things. Especially if I'm mad. I'm glad you know how to protect me. You took care of me. You did the right thing." She smiled. "I don't know what you said to my mother, but it worked."

Then she stepped forward — and I stepped forward — I don't know which of us made the first move and probably we both moved at the same time — and we hugged. First time.

And I was thinking that the most important thing wasn't what I said to her mother. It was what I didn't say. Just as, I remembered, when I first met Kirsten her most important word had been the one she hadn't used.

We stepped back from each other. Everyone was still staring. Kirsten's face had turned sad.

"I'm so sorry about your uncle."

"Yes. Well."

"He was *different*."

"Yes. He was." Thinking of my uncle, I thought of something corny and predictable. "Kirsten?"

"What?"

"May I carry your books?"

She giggled. And she handed them over.

That afternoon, I ran with Kirsten *and* Mrs. Kohler. The air was somewhat turbulent between them, but there were no thunderstorms. Kirsten started to pull ahead, which I knew Mrs. Kohler hated, but when Kirsten saw that I couldn't keep up with her, she slowed down to be with me — and, as it happened, with her mother. Another touchy moment occurred at the end by the lake when Kirsten announced to her mother that she was coming with me to band practice. Mrs. Kohler's only reaction was a long, silent stare. And Kirsten's response was a series of handsprings — which surprised the ducks so much that they retreated to the middle of the lake.

Walking to my house with Kirsten, I told her the band had played "Orangutan." "We made some changes. And — uh — one other thing. They think I wrote it."

"Why didn't you tell them?"

"I thought they might be . . . hostile. Especially Uncle Earl. I wanted them to like the song first."

"Do they like it?"

"Pretty much."

Boone, Dylan, and Law were standing outside the garage when we arrived.

"You could've gone in," I said.

"It's . . . spooky," Boone said.

It was. Uncle Earl's mattress was still pushed up against a wall; his clothes still hung on a rope.

"Creepy," Boone said. "It feels like he's still here."

"He is," Law said, picking up his drumsticks and playing a few bars. "That's him. He showed me that."

Dylan looked surly. "What's *she* doing here?" Nodding at Kirsten.

"I invited her," I said.

"You should've asked us," Dylan said. "It's not just *your* band."

Kirsten looked nervous. She stood slightly behind me as if trying to hide.

"All right," I said. "I'm asking you."

"No," Dylan said.

"What can she do?" Boone asked.

"Piano," Kirsten said, still behind me.

Dylan bristled.

"We've already got Dylan on keyboards," Boone said. "Can you sing?"

"Some," Kirsten said. "I mean I don't take voice lessons or anything, but —"

"Let's try her," Boone said. "We need a singer."

"Yeah," Law said. "For sure."

Since I was the band's singer, this was not exactly a compliment to me.

Dylan looked sulky. But he was outvoted.

We tried "Orangutan." First we played it for her — and she listened, thoughtfully, as if she'd never heard it — and never let on that she'd written it. It didn't seem to bother her that Boone kept flubbing and couldn't even handle a three-note sequence on a bass guitar, though it always bugged the rest of us, especially Dylan.

I gave Kirsten the lyric sheet. As we played again, she sang. Our PA system was just an old hi-fi that I'd patched together with some help from my father. Kirsten's voice came out deeper with the bass jacked up the way we had it. For the first verse, she seemed to be listening to herself, adjusting her pitch, getting used to the sound. Then she let go. She was more expressive than me. More inflection. But still nervous. As she sang, she unconsciously swayed her hips, tapping one hand on her thigh.

Then silence. We all looked at one another.

"Not bad," Boone said.

"Not bad?" Law exclaimed. "That song sounds like it was *made* for her."

"We sorta need a chick," Dylan admitted.

Kirsten flared: "I am *not* a chicken."

Dylan looked surprised. "I mean, you'll give us sex appeal."

Kirsten blushed. I knew what she was thinking: that she didn't have sex appeal, either.

She was going to have a problem getting used to Dylan. Most people do.

"Let's try her," Law said. "See how it goes."

"I can do better," Kirsten said. "This is sort of new to me."

"We can *all* do better," Dylan said, glaring at Boone.

And so, grudgingly, the Four Hairs became Five. Dylan was right: We could all do better.

And we would, I was sure, though it might take a while.

As we were leaving, I mentioned that I wouldn't be coming to school the next day. I'd be attending a memorial service, on a boat, and then we would be scattering Uncle Earl's ashes.

Dylan asked if he could come.

I was surprised, but then when I thought about it, it made sense. I said I didn't see why not.

Then Kirsten asked if she could come. So did Boone. So did Law. And when Danny found out about it later, he wanted to come, too.

They all wanted to pay their respects to Uncle Earl. And, by the way, get out of school.

The boat was a yacht named *Naiad* at Pier 39 near Fisherman's Wharf in San Francisco. To get to her we had to walk past a bunch of T-shirt shops and street musicians. It was like a carnival. A group of harbor seals were lying on a dock nearby. The yacht had wood paneling, big windows, soft chairs. She motored out past Alcatraz Island. In the bay we passed a navy ship that my father said was a minesweeper, and then we passed a containership piled high with metal crates. We were all dressed up. I had fully abluted and was wearing Uncle Earl's shirt, shoes, and tie — knotted the way he'd shown me. We slid under the Golden Gate Bridge. The view was awesome. You could hear the traffic rumbling overhead and the seagulls squealing and the waves thudding on the bow. You could smell the salt and feel the cold spray of water on your face. You could look at the mountains stretching up and down the coast, the red steel understructure of the gigantic bridge, the sparkling white city on the bay. An oil tanker was coming toward us from the ocean — from Alaska.

Besides my friends and my parents, some relatives had come. They all made a point of explaining to me exactly how much I had grown, as if I didn't know. Mrs. Rule was there, too, looking brave and strong — and frowning at my friends for missing school.

Kirsten told me that she had had "a little discussion" with her mother before getting permission to come with me today. I could imagine the heat of that little discussion. But Mrs. Kohler must have decided that I — and my parents — were safe chaperones.

The memorial service was brief, tasteful, and — I thought — very moving. It wasn't particularly religious, which seemed right because Uncle Earl was not a churchgoing person, but it was religious enough to satisfy my mother, who was. We stood gathered at the stern with the wind at our backs. The pilot had cut the motor. We bobbed and drifted. The minister — or whatever he was — read a poem:

Do not stand by my grave and weep
I am not there, I do not sleep.
I am a thousand winds that blow,
I am the diamond glints on snow.
I am the sun on ripened grain,
I am the gentle autumn rain.
When you awake in the morning's hush,
I am the swift uplifting rush of
Quiet birds in circled flight.
I am the stars that shine at night.
Do not stand by my grave and cry,
I am not there, I did not die.

My mother opened the little urn, hesitated a moment, and then cast Uncle Earl's ashes into the air. They swirled and spread and fell into

the Pacific Ocean. Then we each dropped flowers and watched them float away, bright spots
of color in a dull gray sea.

After a few minutes, the engine grumbled
again, and we slowly began to head back to the
bay. Dylan pulled something from under his
jacket. He showed it to me: a scratched-up old
45 rpm record. Chuck Berry. "Brown-Eyed Hand-
some Man." Suddenly he curled his arm and
tossed it like a Frisbee out over the water. It
struck the surface, skipped once, twice, over
some flowers and settled into an oncoming wave.

On the return trip through the bay, a buffet
lunch was served inside the boat. Kirsten and I
stayed at the stern.

"I have to say," Kirsten said, "for a Little
League coach, I didn't like the way he treated
girls."

"Neither did I."

"But if it wasn't for him, I wouldn't have had
a team to play on."

If it wasn't for him, I was thinking, you would
still be in boarding school. Or at least, you
wouldn't be here with me.

It seemed only right that in the end, we gave
him flowers.

"Remember, Kirsten, that first day I met you,

you said that your mother told you that everyone is gifted in their own way?"

"Uh-huh."

"Well, he was gifted, too."

"So are you," Kirsten said.

"So are you," I said.

We looked down at the water, swirling, bub-
bling in the wake.

"I think you may write a song about this,"
Kirsten said.

"I think you may write a poem," I said.

But at that moment, neither of us was writing a word. We looked in each other's eyes, and
what I saw was life and death — a ball of
flame — and pure rock and roll. Walking to the
graveyard, hand in hand. Kissing and stuff. The
chrysalid, cracking its cocoon. Two dragonflies,
soaring to the sun.

APPENDIX

For what it's worth . . . The Songs (and Poems)

DRAGONFLY

Dragonfly, Dragonfly,
Are you friendly? Are you shy?
You turn cartwheels on my shoes,
Make me lose these muddy blues.

Wild as the starry sky,
Blonde of hair and blue of eye,
A thousand freckles, two big ears,
Stay with me a hundred years.

Dragonfly, Dragonfly,
Tell me what and tell me why.
I'm a reptile, juvenile,
Make me human with your smile.

THE VEGETARIAN

Here, piggy
Come, piggy
Stay by me
I'll guard you with machine guns and a
Cup of tea.

Nibble on the slops
Wallow in your hole
I'll save you from becoming
Mama's casserole.

MRS. KOHLER

Here, Kirsten
Come, Kirsten
Stay by me
I'll guard you with machine guns and a
PhD.

Learn your lessons
Watch your posture
Mind your mother, too
I'll save you from a cage in
Babcock's little zoo.

LOVE IS NO GAME

He poured gasoline
On the back tire
And then with a match
He set it on fire.
Do you see the explosion, the bright ball of flame?
Then let me tell you: Love is no game.

They turned their back
To the band
And walked the streets
Hand in hand.
She had hair like a bomb and eyes like the wind
Never was danger so feminine.

Ain't gonna brag
'Bout what I do
Just wanna try
Some stuff with you.

Come to the graveyard with your lips and your
    hair.
I'll show you my love if you show me you dare.

PAPA'S BLUES

Alone in the bedroom, four hours 'til dawn
Rainy day coming, sunny days gone.
Shut up, birds, don't sing me no coos
Light's off in the kitchen, Papa's got blues.

He smiles, he lies, you shake the man's hand
But he'll never tell you just where you stand
Until it's too late, you've got nothing to choose
Light's off in the kitchen, Papa's got blues.

Snake in the night, warm eggs he can steal,
Headlights come at you, drunk at the wheel,
Babies ain't cheap, the lawyer will sue,
Light's off in the kitchen, Papa's got blues.

THE RED CANOE

Took a girl
For a paddle
In my red canoe

Lay there in the sunlight under
Sky
    so
        blue.

See your eyes
See your freckles
See your big ears, too
Of all the people on the planet
I'll
    take
        you.

Chew your hair
Don't you dare
Silly thing to do
Stay here in the sunlight under
Sky
    so
        blue.

MAMA DEAR (by Babcock and Kirsten)

Mama dear
Don't come near
The time has come that we parted.
Baby girl

Now a pearl
Will finish what you started.

Mama dear
Life is queer
Not at all what you planned.
He ain't rough
But he's tough
And with him I will stand.

You can't stop me
He won't drop me
Some things are beyond your control.
My time to run
Yours is done
The young take the place of the old.

UNTITLED (by Kirsten)

I run with you through a forest
where deer nuzzle
at our knees.
Chickadees
nest in our hair.
Little frogs peep
in our pockets.
Wildflowers sprout

313

from our fingers
and ferns from our legs.
Our sweat sprays like rain.
Our lungs blow the wind.
From our eyes
shafts of light
give life
while the beat of our feet
drives the dance
of the forest.

IN THE SCHOOL OF THE ORANGUTAN (by Kirsten)

In the school of the orangutan
The desks are made of mud
The teachers throw the spitballs
They hit you with a thud.

In the school of the orangutan
You work like a computer
A little lady guards your room
Armed with a peashooter.

In the school of the orangutan
The headmistress wears a jock
You sit upon a battery
Wrong answers get a shock.

In the school of the orangutan
They tie your feet with chain
They nail your hands to wooden books
And microwave your brain.

In the school of the orangutan
The only food is meat
On clipboards they write what you eat
And how much you excrete.

In the school of the orangutan
Each day new kids arrive
The buses go home empty
No one gets out alive.

BABA OO MAU MAU (by Kirsten)

Ba ba ba
Ba ba bo
Baba bo, baba bo
Ba ba ba
Ba ba bo
Baba bo, baba bo
Bo booba
Boo boo ba
Booba ba, booba ba
Be be ba

Bum bum bum
Beedle um, beedle um
Be bop a
Boop boop boop
Beedle oop, beedle oop
Ba ba ba
Ba ba bo
Baba Beau Boo Bo.